AF388187

Monday at Ten

A True Story
about Conscious Dying and Love

Carola Gehrke

Printing, binding and distribution: tredition GmbH,
An der Strusbek 10, 22926 Ahrensburg, Germany
Paperback ISBN: 978-3-384-05175-2
ebook ISBN: 978-3-384-05176-9

First edition in German, April 19, 2023:
Original title: Willst Du wirklich sterben, Vater meines
Herzens?—Eine wahre Geschichte
Editing: Natalie Wasserman
Paperback ISBN-13: 978-3750469457
ebook ISBN-10: 3750469458

About the Author

Photo: UMK

Carola Gehrke, born in 1965, studied biology, German literature and pedagogics at the Technical University, Berlin, in order to become a teacher. Early on she realized that her vision of intuitive learning and self empowering students was in opposition with the school system of the time. So instead she focused on completing an MSc in biology at the Friedrich Wilhelm University in Bonn.

During a student expedition to Northern Swedish Lapland, she fell in love with the nature north of the polar circle, and subsequently went on to work as a nature guide and researcher at ANS Abisko Scientific Research Station for five consecutive winters and summers. In cooperation with the Swedish Polar Research Secretariat and BAS British Antarctic Survey, she also participated in research expeditions to the Antarctic and Svalbard. In 1991, she moved to Sweden and obtained her PhD in biology about global climate change effects on arctic and antarctic ecosystems at Lund University and completed a post doc at Copenhagen University.

An ecologist at heart, she's always believed there has to be more to 'the science of life'—which biology signified for her—than experiments and numbers. Already as a teenager, she'd written poetry inspired by nature and had never understood the common separation between the humanities and the natural sciences. For her, the two complement one another and belong together. Leaving 'hard core' science in 2000, she moved to the warmer climate of Los Angeles. As Dean of Doctoral Programs in Integrative Western and Traditional Chinese Medicine at Yo San University, she implemented and developed the curricula and passionately supervised PhD students, facilitating both their integrative research and personal growth.

Since 2013, she has lived in Berlin, resuming her vision of intuitive teaching and developing techniques to simplify learning for her students in Swedish, English, and German. After gaining first hand experience in using energy for healing purposes, she teamed up with a psycho-kinesiologist to explore the complex interplay between the function of the human body, free flow of energy, and processes in the conscious and subconscious mind.

In her spare time, Carola loves strolling around in nature, marveling at its complexity and wonders. Fascinated by ancient cultures, her hobbies include ethnic music, oriental belly dancing, and practicing bow and arrow shooting. She continues to write poetry and short stories, and is working on her first novel.

Preface

Conscious dying? Is it at all possible? And what about conscious living? Can we do one without the other? Where do laughter, joy, pleasure, trust, and truth in the self and others fit in? And what's love got to do with it?

Ulrich was my chosen father; the father of my heart for sixteen years. When his application for assisted dying was granted in July 2022 and we suddenly only had five days left, I had to make decisions: either fight his choice, or accept it; spend time with him until the end, or not. My ultimate journey with him through his final five days and beyond turned out to be an enormous eye-opener and game changer for my entire life. In this book, I invite you to join me in my experience, and maybe also explore some of your own questions and answers!

Regarding how the English version of the book was born... Well, that happened immediately after my book came out in German, on April 19, 2023—nine months to the day of Ulrich's self-chosen assisted passing—when my friend Dani Casselman from Los Angeles, one of my two former homes, inquired as to whether I intended to translate it. Her passion and belief in its success inspired me and drove me forward.

In the following weeks more friends from California, where I'd lived for around sixteen years, turned to me with the same question; they were joined by friends from Sweden, my other former home of almost fourteen years. I realized then that I'd really love to share this story with the people I'd previously spent parts of my life with. And of course, with others too!

In the beginning of June this year, I sat down to translate the first pages into English. To my surprise, I couldn't find the right words. Nothing seemed adequate enough to express the depth and range of emotions, laughter and love, conflicts and solutions; the unexpected twists and turns and the spiritual, light openings that signify this story.

So here I was, fluent in English, having taught it for more than twenty years, in addition to frequently writing and publishing poetry in it; yet I was unable to translate my own book. Well, I figured, I would simply re-write it. Simply! A few days later, on a warm spring night, when all I yearned for was to go on with my life, I called it quits. There was no way I could again dive that deeply into what had happened.

My search for a translator also seemed futile. The few doors that appeared to open closed just as quickly. At the end of August I was about to give up, when a friend connected me with her friend, Becky Beetz. We hit it off from the first phone call. The next day Becky sent me a few translated pages and I immediately recognized and loved my own telling voice. During our second conversation, we cut a win-win deal, spontaneously meeting in person a few days later. Both of us marveled at what a fit it all was. Coincidentally, she was available immediately because her next project was only supposed to start seven weeks later.

At the same time, I received a letter from Dani. In her beautiful handwriting she wrote: "If you need help revising the English translation, let me know!" Overjoyed and humbled, I accepted.

And so our team of three set off! Ever since, the forthcoming text of this English version has been easy, joyful, and pleasurable! Thank you!

In the final phase of the first draft, more team members popped up. Literally. On a hot summer morning when I was editing the final chapters on my laptop, two tiny bundles of meowing fur kept snuggling and clambering all over me on a sofa in an outdoor cafe. They climbed the screen, explored the keyboard, opened the music program, and added some letters here and there to the text. So if you happen to find some extra 'q's, 'x's or 'a's while reading, lucky you! Maybe there's a message hidden right there!

The message the kittens had for me was obvious: hardly a few weeks old, they reminded me of the cycle of life; how birth and death are the gates through which we come and leave, and how precious the ocean of moments that lies in between and beyond is!

So come and travel with me through some of these special moments of the final five days that I had the privilege of spending with Ulrich, right into the opening beyond... where the ultimate end turned out to be nothing but a shift into new beginnings.

For my two fathers!

The one
who called me into this life

And the one
who supported me
in becoming who I truly am

With love

—— * ——

"Be enduring, patient, and silent!"

"I myself shall lead you; love itself shall guide me."

From the libretto of the opera Magic Flute by Wolfgang Amadeus Mozart

Can You Be a Witness?

I'm sitting on my sofa with a large glass of water, tousled hair, and sandy summer feet. It's been an incredible day of sailing. Bright blue skies over Berlin's Havel River. A delicious twenty-five degrees, and fierce gusts of wind blasting from ever-changing directions like wild children around me and my sailing buddy.

My cell phone rings. The name "Ulrich B." pops up on the screen. Happy and tired, I answer, greeting him with "Hi Ulrich" as I do every evening when we call to check in on each other and see how the day has been. A few moments of small talk. Things like, "How was your lunch?" and "Have you been down to the Branitzer today?"

The Branitzer. A square surrounded by mighty chestnut trees in Berlin's Westend where Ulrich makes his rounds each day. Only in company and with breaks on one of the many benches. When he feels stronger, he even adds a second round.

Today though, it's different.

"At last," says Ulrich agitatedly, indignant even. "Are you coming on Monday at ten?" he asks, his voice strained. "Can you be a witness?" "Huh? Excuse me? Witness? To what?" "To my passing."

My brow furrows. "Um, what? What for??" I ask again. This must be one of his jokes and I'm waiting for his chuckle. But it's futile. I don't want to be reminded of what this might be about, but I am—and I'm left breathless.

This can't be my life, I think, and I recall how I was taken aback at the beginning of the year when I learned that, with the support of his family, Ulrich had applied to a German organization for assisted dying. I made it clear at the time I would stay out of the matter, and was reassured that a decision on his application could only be made after six months at the earliest.

"You always talked about fall, about September... October," I stammer, horrified. "It hasn't even been six months yet." Why doesn't he say anything? "No," he persists. "No, it's now. On Monday. At ten."

I'm speechless. Maybe I've misheard him and my silence will swallow his words like a black hole; a meadow full of flowers blooming in its place. So that everything will stay the same. Like it was a few minutes ago. When I just wanted to rest on my sofa, intoxicated and tired from the wind, water, and sun; to share the great day with him, the sailor of so many oceans, before I go to bed early in order to wake up refreshed to another summer's day. A few minutes ago. When life was still infinite. When everything was still open. Blue skies over Berlin's Havel.

Pressing my cell phone to my ear, I look at the clock. It is 7.37 p.m. As tears well up in my eyes, I choke out, "Ulrich... Please... Can I come over?" "Yes," he says, clearly relieved. "Yes." And "Good. Very good. Come quickly."

I drop everything—even my tiredness, my exhaustion. At least I remember to lock the door to my balcony. I reach for my apartment keys, bicycle helmet, saddle protector. As I go to grab my bag too, my helmet and keys slip out my hands and clatter to the floor.

All of a sudden, shock and fear are running through my limbs. A terrible feeling grows in my stomach as if I'm hurtling downhill on a rollercoaster. Instability and a sense of no longer having any control over existence bear down on me like an avalanche. I won't let it happen. I pull on my helmet, cling more tightly to my possessions, and slam my apartment door behind me. I cover the seven-minute bike ride through the streets of Berlin's Westend in less than four—running two red lights along the way. In front of Ulrich's front door I gasp for air while I press the doorbell. Immediately he lets me in. He must've been waiting at the door, I think. Taking the stairs two at a time, I race to the second floor.

As I round the stairwell's last curve, I see him. Ulrich. Standing there. Leaning on his cane, swaying, rather like a lonely sailing ship on a motionless ocean. From his still clear blue eyes, which have seen ninety-seven years of life, he's beaming at me. Just like always. A lighthouse in my life. His eyes, his face, indeed his whole body, seem to glow. A sight that makes me feel as helplessly warm, wide and open as ever—even now as I notice a fearful uncertainty in his eyes. I stop, soaking up his appearance with my own. Tears stream down my face. He won't be standing here like this much longer. How can I bear it?

I jump the last few steps, throw my things on the hall dresser, and give him a long hug. Just like always. We sit down, as always, in his dining room; Ulrich to the right of the head of the long dining table, and I at the corner to his left. We talk at length. At some point his crutch, which is leaning against the chair, slips and hits the floor. His rage flares. He tries to take a sip of water. As he does so, the glass slips out of his trembling hands before I can catch it, and a pool of water spills across the table. "Ulrich! Oh Ulrich!" he scolds himself. "Ulrich! Dear Ulrich!" I beseech, trying to reassure him. "It's not your fault. Please... don't be so hard on yourself...!" But in his acts of strict self-discipline, he's unreachable. Like always—and somehow this is comforting.

I hold his hands. Or is he holding mine? Who knows. My questions, naked and raw, lurking like hungry mouths, jump on Ulrich. They find no answer, but feel heard. We talk for a long time.

About how glad he is that I've come. About how horrified I am that his application for assisted dying has been approved. And moreover, so quickly. I never would've expected that. Never ever. That they would even grant it. It enrages me.

I sob over why it has to happen so quickly. He's doing well now. Or at least much better. He speaks about the quiet parts of his life, of when the food slips from his trembling fork; of when he doesn't know whether in the next moment a fainting spell will rob him of his strength and cause him to fall, as he so often does. I know about these details. We've talked about them many times. For months I took turns with others, supporting him in his daily life.

"Ninety-seven!" he suddenly splutters in anger—or is it horror? "My God, I'm ninety-seven!" And then: "That's no life. And it won't get any better."

Eventually, all has been said, all tears have been shed, and our hands have been held enough. What I don't dare to say is, "Please... please, stay a little longer." Because I know it won't change anything. Instead, I say, "I'm going home now to sleep." Ulrich nods and, using his walker for support, accompanies me to the door. Like always.

Before we embrace, as we do each time, the one withheld question bursts out of him: "Do you understand me, Carola?" And again: "Do you understand me?" I look at him. His pleading eyes. I feel his despair at what life has become after so many fulfilling years. I feel his internal resolve wavering. My heart aches. Isn't it more important that he understands himself? A wave of love bursts from my heart as I face him earnestly, steadfastly. "Yes, Ulrich. Yes, I understand you." And I mean it. Every word. At least I do in this moment.

I feel the tension escaping from his body, how he's becoming smaller again, weaker. How exhausting life is for him. We hold each other for a long time, recharging. Tears are streaming from my eyes because I realize that our father-daughter hugs are now numbered. As we face one another again, apart, we go through our intimate ritual, established many years ago. We place our palms in front of our chests. In front of our hearts.

I bow to him. "Mr. B." He bows back. "Doctor."

"Sleep well, Ulrich! See you tomorrow!" "Are you coming tomorrow?" he asks, his voice uncertain. "Yes," I reply in a surprisingly firm voice. "Yes! I'll be with you tomorrow afternoon at two. When your nurse leaves." Never before have I been so sure of myself. I will be there. He smiles. "Good!" he says, "Very good!"

Slowly I descend the stairs, trying to be as I used to be—but I can't. As I push open the heavy front door, I'm swallowed by the unashamedly balmy summer evening. I take my bike, put my helmet in the basket, and want to get going—but it's all too quick. Actually everything goes too fast for me.

I look at my calendar. July. Fourteen, fifteen, sixteen, seventeen, eighteen. As I push my bike, I begin to calculate. And then I burst into tears, unrestrained, and without a helmet, under the chestnut and linden trees that Ulrich loves as much as I do.

We only have five days.

The Number Five

After the initial shock, I never could've imagined that a 'five' could instill in me such peace, such hope. At least, that is, until I unlock my front door. Secure within my own four walls, I realize for a brief moment, like lightning striking sharply, what's coming. A fog creeps in, lulling me with the number five. We still have five more days and there's only one thing that matters: that I spend every single afternoon and evening with Ulrich.

But what will we do? How will we spend this precious time that is both so final and so short? Five days seem to be all at once irrevocably brutal and unnecessarily miserly. The question usually is: "What would you do if you had five days, four days, three days, two days, one day left to live?"

I've never heard anyone ask, "What if a person you're close to only had five days left—until Monday at ten o'clock to be exact—because they've decided to end their life? How would you want to spend your time together? What would you say to each other? What would you keep silent?"

Blindsided, I'd agreed to his request. Of course I'd be a witness. At the same time, I feel queasier by the minute. "No!" everything inside me is screaming. "No!

No! No!" Do I really want to do this to myself, to watch my chosen father take his own life? Because that's what it is, plainly said. A suicide, as it's clinically labelled. A self-murder. Albeit one that's medically approved and, on the top, medically assisted. But where and what is 'the Self'? And does 'the Self' actually die when the body ceases to live? I also have no clue what this process involves. Will the doctor inject Ulrich with something?

Wrapped in a light shawl, I step onto my balcony, and look up at the night sky. It's gathering thick clouds, foretelling the thunderstorm that has been raging in my brain since Ulrich's call. Shocked, I agreed at first, because I didn't want to leave Ulrich alone with this wish in his last moments. Though if I'm honest, I also agreed because I want to hoard all the minutes we can spend together. Like a squirrel with its nuts, I want to store them in a safe place for the hard times that will follow.

In the last six months, Ulrich has been on the brink of death so many times. I've said goodbye to him, and we've said goodbye to each other so many times, that his dying already feels a bit drained. A bit used up. Only now do I understand what the phrase 'It's serious' really means.

In the past, I've asked Ulrich if he wants to be alone when he dies. The man, who has been so content to spend time by himself during his long life, has always surprised me anew with his answer: "No. I want you to be with me." I wonder when the Steppenwolf had turned into a crane. Still free and full of self-confidence, but now also seeking companionship for his last journey.

Confused, I sip a glass of water, seeking comfort and answers in its cool wetness. I need to talk to someone. Automatically I reach for my cell phone to dial Ulrich's number. For it was he, this man in his mid-nineties, who I've turned to in the last two years when I thought I was all alone in the world; when everything around me seemed to collapse. Like when my mother died and, at the same time, my boyfriend and I separated; when I felt lost many an evening and called Ulrich close to tears.

"Can I come over?" "Of course!" he'd reply. It's the tone, the melody in his voice, that ends up opening wide like his arms, welcoming me in. Every time. A song, a refrain between the verses of my life when I stumble, that holds me with its words alone before I even enter Ulrich's apartment. "Of course!" Then he'd let me come to him, sitting down next to me, listening to me, letting me cry and saying, "I understand you" stroking my hand or my hair while I buried my head in his shoulder, sobbing.

Now more than ever, I need his support. But now he's the one turning my life upside down and can no longer be my confidant. It's in this moment I realize, with shock, how empty my life really is in terms of close friends. The hitherto unique good fortune of being able to enjoy the support of my father, the one that I'd chosen as an adult woman, has been reversed. My life will change; it will have to change, and somehow—yes—somehow that's also a good thing!

Despite the late hour, I call a friend. Then another. One is so at peace with the cycle of birth and death, coming and going, that I can rest in it with her for a moment. She reminds me of myself. Relieved, I hang up. But immediately the fear of Monday washes over me again. The other friend is outraged. How could Ulrich do this to me, leave me, the daughter of his heart, like this? She insists that for love's sake he should, indeed must, decide to stay until a natural death takes him. Should? Must? With each of her words the distance between us grows. My lifelong inner commitment to the free will of every human being makes me abruptly end the conversation. At least I know better now where I stand. Certainly on the edge of a yawning abyss. But also ready to fly.

With that inner clarity I go to bed and sink into a deep, exhausted sleep. A few minutes later though I wake with a jolt, horrified and with intense fear in the pit of my stomach without being able to recall why. Like drowning, flailing wildly in the raging waters of emotions that seem to have no reason, searching for something I can grasp, comprehend; something that could give this emotional chaos a logic, a meaning, and thus a foothold. When the memory suddenly comes back to me, I grab it and pull myself ashore. This one is called Ulrich and Monday and Oh My God. But at least the confusion inside me makes some sense now.

— 25 —

Dropping an anchor, I decide at this moment to write a story—this story.

The First Day

*O*n the morning of the first day, I wake up feeling surprisingly rested considering the situation. However, as I slowly come to, an abyss of unspeakable loneliness cracks my chest wide open. I pull myself together and open the blinds. Innocently, the new day shines in my face. The first of five.

While brewing my morning tea, I write several messages canceling all my afternoon and evening appointments for the next five days. Time is all I have, and I need it for Ulrich and me. Every single minute.

Lastly, I call my naturopath to ask if she's available to see me next Monday afternoon. I carefully record my 5 p.m. appointment with her in my calendar. I want to meet someone who's not been involved in the process when it's over on Monday. 'It'. What do I call 'it'? How do you describe what's happening? Ulrich dying? Ulrich taking his own life? Monday at ten is his 'appointment'. I leave this space empty in my calendar.

On the one hand, I'm at a loss for words. On the other, I'm afraid I might miss 'it' without a reminder. That I'll simply block 'it' out. But that feels even more awful than actually going to Ulrich's on Monday at ten. My recurring dilemma. Do I want to be there when he dies? My schedule keeps taunting me. I realize the answer—the solution to my conflict—isn't to be found in my calendar. In my confusion, I'm beginning to understand that I'm involved in something I have no comprehension of, no answer for. That I have no choice but to trust that somehow I'll be guided. That nothing important will be forgotten, nothing essential will be lost. So I let go.

Fall. Right into the middle of a process that has long since begun.

As I begin my morning yoga, the situation hits me anew and tears start to flow. Sobbing, I bow to the four directions—North, South, East and West—connect with their energies and finally ask for cosmic support for these next five days. And of course for day X. For me, for Ulrich, and for whatever may happen. The idea of offering the universe a dirty deal based on the principle, *If Ulrich changes his mind, then I promise I'll always...* I don't even entertain. Not once has such a thought passed through my mind. Not only because it's his life, his decision, which I'm gradually learning to respect, but because I fear the possible consequences of such a deal.

Indeed, there's another voice inside me whispering, "I can't take it any longer." That bottomless fear, the panic, every time my cell phone rings. The anxious listening for a call half asleep at night. Has he fallen again? Is he dying right now? No more getting up in the morning exhausted. Even if Ulrich is doing better just now. Never again having to know he's suffering, isolated, in hospital. Finally being able to sleep peacefully again, to live quietly. I'm ashamed of this voice and I can't—I don't even want to—silence it.

I promise to take extra good care of myself during the coming five days. First I cycle to the organic food store and fill my basket with things that support my strength and joy. Among them, two handfuls of bright orange-yellow apricots, three bars of my favorite dark chocolate, and a bottle of earthy red wine from grapes grown under the fiery sun in the Spanish south. The latter to toast life with Ulrich. To life in general. But especially his! That's what we talked about yesterday.

On my way home, my bike fully laden, I round the corner from where I can see Ulrich's home. Something compels me to dismount and become conscious of the fact he's there. Still there. I cautiously savor the 'Here', the 'Now', and it feels surprisingly comforting. Infinitely more so than my thoughts of trying to survive the near future by means of plans and appointments.

The corny phrase 'living in the moment' is taking on a real and practical relevance for me. With a deep sigh of relief, I'm letting go of the future and landing on the ground of all that is right now. Ulrich over there and my bike under me. I bathe, even wallow, in the self-evident, which has completely disappeared from my everyday life—namely in a feeling of security, simply because Ulrich, the father of my heart, is living just around the corner. I linger some more, and then the traffic lights turn green.

After I've unpacked my purchases at home, my basket stares at me. It's outrageously empty. Way too empty. Such a void is too much for me, reminds me of something I don't want to think about until it actually happens. Ulrich's passing, as he calls it. The carousel in my head picks up speed again. This time I flee to a lake close to my apartment, fifteen minutes downhill by bike, and let the cold water shock me back into the present. I want to forget, for a single moment, that I'll be starting my first afternoon with Ulrich in just under two hours. The feeling of the last few months—where the afternoons saw me taking over from someone else as a caregiver, albeit with love—has vanished without a trace; my nursing work has abruptly ended. From now on, I'm once again a daughter of the heart, who lends a hand, supports, is there. No more and no less.

Shortly after two, I ring Ulrich's doorbell with a sinking feeling. How will it be? Suddenly it frightens me that so many hours lie ahead of us. What on earth are we going to do? His nurse opens the door with red puffy eyes, seeking my gaze, and instantly begins to cry. My armor goes up. As much as I like and appreciate her—after all, in the spring, we shared Ulrich's caretaking for weeks in harmonious cooperation, she the mornings, I the afternoons and, if necessary, the nights too—I have no consolation to offer her now. I also don't want to get wrapped up in her emotional drama. I have my own to deal with. I smile at her and rush into the living room where Ulrich is waiting for me on a chair at the head of his dining table. As always, he's immaculately dressed, his scarf matching his shirt. "Old people are not a pretty sight," he likes to say. "You have to make an extra effort." And how well he succeeds every day!

"Hello Ulrich!" His expression brightens as I kiss him on the forehead and give his back a firm rub. "Oh, so good you're here!" he exclaims, and "Drama! Drama!" nodding in the direction of the hallway where his nurse is preparing to leave. "Have you been downstairs yet?" I ask, hoping to exchange the oppressive mood in the room for the company of the chestnut trees in Branitzer Square. "Yes," he says, "we've been down. And that's enough for today." So I sit down with him. His nurse, who has since regained her composure, bids us farewell with a pained expression, but also with a kiss for him: "See you tomorrow, Ulrich!" "See you tomorrow," he chirps casually, happily even, and at the same time so forced that it takes me a lot of effort not to shake him hard. What a farce!

Alone at last, we begin to argue. Tough. Fierce. About the reasons, the when, the how of his decision.

Two unequal fighters. He's in charge, I'm pulling up at the rear. I poke. I provoke. Why now? Why not in the fall, like he's been talking about since last year? He evades my questions. Thank God Ulrich spares me the litany this time that he would've shot himself long ago if his gun hadn't been stolen after the Second World War. With such unflinching aggression in his words, this man, so full of life and contentment, has always duped me, massacred me, and ultimately muzzled me. Today, however, he refrains from the dreaded tried and tested blow. Just as we are tangling each other afresh with questions and arguments, and the situation seems most hopeless, his face suddenly becomes soft and vulnerable. His voice trembles as he confesses: "I don't have the courage to grow old, Carola."

Against my will, I'm laughing. "You're ninety-seven years old, Ulrich!" He starts to laugh too and corrects: "I don't have the courage to get any older. Carola, I'm ninety-seven! And it's not getting any better. I don't want to have to move into a residential home someday." That hits me harder than anything else. He, one of the bravest people I know, sailed the seven seas, escaped from French captivity back to Berlin with a homemade compass, and established a highly respected lumber and undertaking business. When Ulrich says he has no more courage, it's serious. I have to close my eyes, so unbearable is his fear of the future. Flooded with sympathy and love, I let go. Laying down his arms, he's won our battle without leaving me feeling like a loser.

A soothing silence falls between us. I put my hand over his trembling fingers and squeeze them ever so gently. All right. Monday. At ten.

I help Ulrich over to his TV chair, slide a footstool under his legs, spread a blanket over him, and lie down on the couch opposite. So many times over the past two years I've napped on this couch, my oasis from the hustle and bustle of everyday life, while Ulrich sat at the table, musing, meditating, and above all, guarding my sleep. Today we're both exhausted. Still, I can't doze off. I listen to his breathing like a comforting symphony of which I don't want to miss a single note.

Every now and then I squint at him, watching him sleep, so peaceful, his cheeks rosy, alive through and through. How bright are cheeks allowed to glow when one wants to die?

As Ulrich begins to move restlessly in his chair, I make us coffee and place the cookie jar on the dining room table. "We're ready to go," I say, beckoning him to join me. As usual, he forgets himself, jumps up and I have to run to him, catching him just in time, before he falls. "Slowly, slowly, Mr. B.!" "Oh yes!" he chuckles while I park his walker in front of him, both of us smiling. After coffee, we move to the glazed balcony, its windows flung wide open. Ulrich sits next to me, his eyes closed and smiling broadly at the warm afternoon sun. Two huge chestnut trees stretch up high into the blue sky in front of us. I too close my eyes, the question of how I got into this strange situation with him in the first place rumbling around inside me.

Interrupting the peace, I ask Ulrich, "How long have we known each other?" He turns his head towards me. "Long," he grins, "a long time!" I nod. "It was 2006," I say. "In June. I was forty then. My goodness, that was sixteen years ago! That's when you were... wait a minute... you must've been eighty." Numbers don't seem to interest him much. "I was visiting Berlin for a month, for the World Cup. Remember?" I nudge him in the side, "one more breath of German air before I moved from Sweden to California. I'd arranged to meet Mom and you were sitting next to her on a bench on the banks of the River Havel. Straight away you jumped up, took my hand as if we were undertaking a formal proposal, and introduced yourself: *Ulrich B.* All that was missing was a kiss on the hand," I laugh, "and do you remember, you then fetched a rickety chair from the shed? You wiped it down and offered me your seat on the bench while you took the wobbly chair. I was flabbergasted. You know, I felt instantly respected and valued by you." He looks at me in amazement, "But of course! What else?" I consider this for a moment. Yes, what else?

"Everything changed with you in my life. Usually, I was never able to stand Mom for long. Somehow, I always felt both guilty and responsible for her wellbeing. Nothing I did was ever enough for her. With you there, I felt supported. Stronger. More free somehow. More independent." Ulrich says nothing. Is he listening? I know very well that he's never really understood my difficulties with my mother. He himself, content with life, was immune to the vast majority of her attempts to make him responsible for her happiness.

"And then you showed me your sailing boat. I was so impressed that you'd built the interior of the Pegasus yourself. So meticulously and lovingly... the way the mahogany wood shone. What a job that must've been!" Ulrich nods. "I worked on it at my lumberyard for a few years. After the Second World War." "Oh right, you had direct access to wood and tools through your lumber business. Anyway, when we first met, I took a picture of you and Mom in front of the bow of the Pegasus. A few months later in Los Angeles, I held the picture in my hands. I sent it to Mom so that she could give it to you. Yes—and that's how our contact began. You called me and thanked me. I was floored. Then we began talking on the phone regularly," I say, rummaging through my memories until I realize Ulrich is only half listening.

"And then what happened?" I try to draw him in. Ulrich shrugs, "I don't remember." "Neither do I," I laugh, "and it doesn't really matter! Anyway, we're sitting here together now. But I do remember that from then on, we talked on the phone. Several times a week. And for long. I remember how you always encouraged me when I didn't know what to do. My eternal dilemma, whether to return to Berlin or not. *You have to fight*, you used to say. And *you just have to want to.* Honestly, Ulrich, I still don't understand the concept. To have to force myself to want? But it doesn't matter. I guess it has to do with your own life experience. However, it meant a lot that you were there for me. That you wanted to know how I was doing." "Sure! You're my daughter!" he says in a voice implying that there's nothing more natural in the world.

"I remember once I was sick and you read me something over the phone. Do you remember that poem about the morning? Hang on a sec, how did it go? Oh yes, *I wish you a good morning, a few…*" Ulrich jumps in "*a few minutes just for you!*" I continue, "*What's coming is still hidden, only…*" Ulrich smiles warmly and softly "*… only rays of sunshine showing through!*" I glow and continue to spin the thread further, "*Maybe you'll have a lovely day, as you hoped it would be…*" And right in the middle of the last line he joins me and we finish the morning greeting together: "*Maybe it'll even make you grow, but that's for you alone to know!*"

The sun disappears behind clouds; it's getting cooler. I pull a blanket over Ulrich's legs. "Is this ok?" He nods, satisfied. "Well, the second time we met was the following summer. I was visiting Berlin again. This time from Los Angeles. I'd arranged to meet Mom and you. For the first time together. Like a little family! Both of you were going to pick me up at the Zehlendorf train station. When I climbed the stairs, I saw you standing there at the entrance. You were wearing an open corduroy jacket over your azure blue shirt. The image has been burned into my memory. Instead of waiting for me in the car with Mom, you came to the stairs to greet me. You picked me up. I was so touched by that." Again Ulrich looks over at me. Puzzled. "Yes, of course! It was a given!" Again, as if that was the only option. Though somewhere deep inside me it hurts like hell and I understand that I owe this white-haired man next to me with the blanket over his legs the fatherhood I've longed for all my life.

"Do you know how important you are to me?" It's not the first time I've asked him this in the two years since my mother died. Ulrich nods a resounding yes. A lump forms in my throat. "What's it going to be like when you're not here anymore?" I choke out, tears streaming down my face.

Ulrich takes my hand, stroking it. "It's true, you don't have any family to support you." So simple, this truth. This is exactly what I both hate and also love about him: that clarity, the courage to name things as they arc. How alike we are in this.

I'm crying uncontrollably, feeling infinitely abandoned and lost, like an orphan. He simply sits with me, stroking my hand with his tender, trembling fingers, and that makes me cry even more. This loving, accepting, quiet way of just being with me in such moments is precisely what makes him special for me—the father who understands my heart. Because that's what this coming Monday is for me. Really, really devastating. I grieve a bit in advance, now, while he's still here and it's still possible for him to hold my hand as only he can. Yes, he knows very well what he means to me. And still, he's decided to leave. At this thought, anger flares up in me, shooting like lightning; quenched by a flood of tears. Initially, at least. Because I realize that my anger at his decision to die on Monday will eventually claim its rightful space. And also that he bears no responsibility for me, and my feeling of being an orphan from yesteryear.

"Do you remember how you and Mom picked me up at Tegel Airport during the years I visited Berlin?" I say, rowing myself out of the sea of tears. "I so enjoyed seeing you two standing there at the gate. So naturally. Just like parents. And I was welcome!" Before the next 'Yes, of course, what else' can cross Ulrich's lips, I continue, "and then I stayed with you every time." Out of the blue Ulrich becomes irritated. "At one point you lived with me for a really long time! Far too long —half a year," he grumbles. There it is. The truth. Again. The blood rushes to my face. "Yes, in February 2013, when I arrived in Berlin, my birthplace, with all my luggage in my hands, trying to figure out what I was still searching for here in Berlin. I had given up everything in Los Angeles. My everyday life. My job. My home. My car. I wanted to find an apartment in Berlin and... hmm, what? As soon as I arrived at the airport with my seven suitcases, I knew it was a mistake. For half a year I didn't get anything done..." I remember. "It was terrible... I was homesick for California, the Pacific Ocean, the mountains... And your eternal *'You wanted it that way'* only made things worse. Ulrich shrugs his shoulders.

"You were always sitting with that thing at the dining room table," he wrinkles his nose as if my laptop, which I was working on at the time, were something deeply indecent, "and I thought you'd at least cook once in a while." His accusation still stings, so unbearable it is that he'd been disappointed in me. "I did!" I snap, "you just didn't like my food." "Yes, when you cook weird stuff, like you did," he counters sharply. I cannot help but laugh. "Hmm, it might have tasted funny to YOU. But not to me and my friends. You only like traditional German cooking, and I like vegetarian food!"

He keeps teasing me. "You were obnoxious!" "And so were you!" Clumsily we laugh. "And then I kicked you out. One more month, I told you, and then you're moving out!" I let that sink in for a moment. "Yes," I confess, "it was just as well. I needed to go back to California and make a fresh start there. But it was pretty tough to suddenly be handed a moving-out date by you of all people! I never thought we'd make up. I never ever wanted to see you again," I retort playfully, trying to sound huffy. "But just a week after I'd moved out, I made a calendar with pictures from those six months for you... as a thank you for my time with you." A warm smile floods Ulrich's face. We squeeze each other's hands, glad that it's all in the past. Just two years ago, right after my mom had passed, Ulrich assured me, as if to provide comfort, "You always have a home here with me!"

Have we ever really gotten along? In everyday matters—not at all! Politically, too, we thought the other to be completely derailed. And we still do. I can't help but laugh again. "Actually, Ulrich, I think it's only now in the last two years that we've really found each other as father and daughter! It wasn't until after Mom died that I started to feel free and relaxed enough to come to you whenever I liked. She was jealous of everything and everyone I spent time with." Ulrich looks at me in amazement. It's incredible to me that he didn't notice that.

"Your mother's passing—that was a terrible blow for me," Ulrich says, mountains of sadness in his voice. I close my eyes as his pain touches mine. "I know," I nod, "you had a task then, and you two knew each other for so long. Thirty years or so?" I ask. "About that. It's terrible when everyone around you passes away. For a few years, I was at times attending several funerals a month," Ulrich recalls thoughtfully, "and your mother's was one of the last." I sigh and wonder what it would be like if the people who matter to me all vanished. If there was no one my age, in my generation, left to reminisce with. Be it just about my favorite TV series that I used to watch when I was a girl—Sandman or Wickie—or milestones like the fall of the Berlin Wall or the turn of the millennium.

Even now, when I think about it, I don't really have anyone I can remember my research trips with, for example. The silky veils of the Polar northern lights flickering silently or blowing wildly; huskies pulling sleds while barking deafeningly and howling under a billion stars across a deep, frozen, cracking lake; thundering, towering glaciers; king penguins calling out for each other like donkeys and belching elephant seals with their huge flared noses in the mud pools of the Antarctica. My colleagues from back then are scattered far and wide. "Yes, I understand," I say thoughtfully, "it feels truly lonely."

"Do you know how much it helped me when you visited Mom in her retirement home every afternoon and I knew that someone was with her? For the first time in my life, I was free to decide when I really wanted to see her." "I always went to see her at three," Ulrich remembers, "it was only three blocks from here. Mostly we solved riddles. In the last few weeks before she died though, she slept a lot and I just sat with her." For a moment I'm tempted to remind him that I was the only one permitted to see her in the last six weeks leading up to her death, but somehow it doesn't matter. Even during the many, many months before this, my mother would often doze off when visitors were there. The image brings tears to my eyes. "Yes, it was good for all three of us. Now you're the only person in my life who has known Mom for so long and so closely," I suddenly realize. "My goodness, Ulrich, my last earthly connection with my mother is with you..." Ulrich nods, his lips tightly closed, and I wipe tears from my eyes all over again.

"Remember how you ended up in an inpatient clinic for physiotherapy around the corner from me last year after fracturing your thigh?" Ulrich grunts, "Oh, my God, that was excruciating! They just left me lying there for weeks in the room," he shakes his head fiercely, "and no one was allowed to see me. Terrible!" "Yes, I know," I murmur, "only once did they let me in to visit. You'd become terribly shaky and skinny. I could hardly stand to see how fragile you were. I didn't believe you'd ever come home again. Never ever! When you suddenly discharged yourself from the clinic just one day later..." "About time," he interrupts me in an excited voice. "... you scared the hell out of me. I was so mad... I didn't believe you'd manage a day without round-the-clock help! And that I would be constantly torn out of my life and have to step in..." I erupt. Ulrich looks at me with wide eyes. His voice confident as ever, he answers: "But why would you even think this way?"

The innocent astonishment in his voice shames me deeply. It's true. Because I'd completely underestimated him. This incredible strength he would draw from within himself over and over again. And which keeps attracting people who can't help but give him their love and care.

Including me. Even at the age of ninety-seven. "Such an old man I am!" he exclaimed many times, amazed, bewildered even, at the constant sea of flowers adorning his dining room table. My admiration for this man knows no limits.

Contemplative, I recap the hours before his fall, which led to the fracture and surgery a good two years ago. I'd told him on the phone that my mom would certainly prefer light-colored clothes for her funeral—after all, she'd complained all her life about the depressingly dark dress code at burials. Ulrich, who as an undertaker had organized funerals and delivered eulogies for decades through his own renowned institute, had exploded in a fit of rage. He would wear black, he'd ranted at the other end of the line. "Fine," I'd replied, "then you wear black." No, he'd continued to rant and rave, it wouldn't work at all if I wore light colored clothes, because if he walked next to me behind the urn, we'd look like a wedding couple. So, he would walk at the very back. I'd had trouble holding back my laughter. "Fine," I'd conceded, "then you'll walk at the back." Before I could finish my next sentence—"But let's talk about it more later"—he'd already angrily broken off the conversation. A short while after, he'd called back. His voice had sounded subdued, fragile even. He'd had a bad fall and the ambulance was already on its way over. At first I felt terribly guilty, without reason. But now that this is all history, I dare to ask him: "And—was it worth it?" Ulrich understands immediately and shakes his head. "No!" he grins.

After that, Ulrich had managed well and with little help for a whole year. Then last October they suddenly started. The phone calls. His terrified, shaky voice: "Carola! I've fallen again!" "Do you want me to come over?" I'd ask. "Yes, please!" If possible I went directly to him, took him in my arms, gave him a glass of water, cleaned his wounds, and stuck band-aids on, if he hadn't already treated himself. With a few exceptions, he was able to get up on his own.

Half a century of morning exercise had made him, to this day, incredibly agile, flexible, and strong in body. To my amazement, it only ever took him a few days to fully recover from his falls. What remained, however, was a fear that it could happen again at any moment. That suddenly everything would turn. That his legs would just give way. Like pudding.

"When I think about the bruises you've gotten from falling in the last six months. Whole landscapes of contusions. And how quickly they always healed. My goodness," I gently stroke Ulrich's delicate fingers, "even your hands look so young. No lumps. Nothing!" "Well!" beams the father of my heart, "autogenic training!" I have to smile. How alike we are. It's our lives and it's us who are leading them.

"When did you start with autogenic training?" "Hmm... that was more than fifty years ago." "Fifty years? And since then, you've been doing it every day?" Ulrich nods, "Sometimes several times a day." Holy discipline! "It's incredible how you've steered your body into healing mode time and again." "It's very simple. I start in silence. Thinking about nothing. Wanting nothing. Forcing nothing. And nowadays, I just need to start with the first few words to immediately and completely relax. Then I tell my body exactly what to do: *The heart is beating strongly and evenly. All organs are working harmoniously with one another. The skin is firm, elastic, and optimally supplied with blood. The tissue is optimally supplied with oxygen.* And so on. That's how I also direct my energy to where I've injured myself."

"How long does one round of autogenic training take?" "Depends. I always do it before I get up. Sometimes I'm done in twenty minutes. But there have been other times… when I felt really light," he beams. "I rose higher and higher, like a feather. Sometimes I floated high above my body. Until suddenly there was a jolt… and swiiish," he whistles through his teeth, "… I came down again, back into my body. *What a pity!* I always thought, *Too bad, it was so beautiful!*"

"Yes, you're good with heights!" I grin. "Remember when your boat's wind indicator got stuck on one of our sailing trips?" Ulrich looks at me questioningly. "To fix it, you steered the Pegasus to the lifting crane at the jetty. After I moored the boat, you were suddenly nowhere to be seen. I was really worried—until I heard your voice from above: *Carola, I can't reach the mast! Lean over the railing and tilt the boat a bit!* Quick as a weasel at the age of eighty, you'd scaled the mast, holding on to it seven meters above me with one hand, trying to reach the top with the other. Did you notice how the other sailors rushed over and stared up, open-mouthed at you?" Ulrich chuckles in amusement. "You laugh, but I almost had a heart attack!"

"Gee, it was hard for me to sell the Pegasus!" sighs Ulrich. "You were in your mid-eighties, right?" Ulrich looks sorrowful. "Well, it had to end at some point." "You enjoyed trips on the River Havel with her for so many decades. Plus you cruised the Mediterranean and went all the way to the Panama Canal in chartered sailing boats...!" "That was in the sixties," Ulrich interrupts me thoughtfully, "you can't even imagine the circumstances and primitive conditions from back then."

"And your first boat?" "It was a small sailing dinghy I found on the lakeside when I was a boy." "When you were at boarding school?" "Yes. The boat was rotten, unusable. But I liked it. So I searched for the owner and asked how much he wanted for it. Twenty German marks! Can you imagine? I offered him five, but he just laughed at me." Ulrich looks at me with eyes wide open. "*There's nothing to laugh about*, I told him, *five marks is all I have.*" "And...?" "He let me have it for five marks." Ulrich was just eleven, but what touches me the most is that even today, all this is simply a matter of course for him.

After all that has been talked about, the rest of the evening rolls along lazily. A call from his nurse is the only interruption: she wants to make sure Ulrich's doing okay. And she makes another attempt to persuade him to continue living. It visibly strains him, challenges him. But he says no.

Around 10 p.m., I help him with his evening hygiene routine. We're a well-rehearsed team, laughing, amusing ourselves with the banalities and absurdities of physical existence. I help him into his pajamas and carefully wrap the blanket around him. Innocent as a little boy, he looks at me. "So, Skipper, now the equipment check before going to sleep!" I prompt him, because he avoids getting up at night when he's alone in the apartment. "Alarm clock?" Ulrich nods. The digital neon numbers are clearly visible to him from his bed. "Water?" Ulrich nods towards the orange cup, which is filled and sitting on his nightstand. "And the Mercedes is right here by the bed, waiting for you! Please, please don't run off without it in case you do have to get up," I remind the grinning Ulrich of his walker.

"Lots of love, Ulrich!" I place my hand on my heart. With my other hand, I trace circles on the blanket over his chest. "Yes... oh yes..." he murmurs with a sleepy smile. "Sleep well, Ulrich. See you tomorrow."

As quickly and quietly as possible, I tidy up the kitchen and trundle home. So that's how it was. Our first last day. I didn't expect anything and yet I'm completely surprised. How ordinary and normal it was, and yet so very different and special. It gives me courage for what's to come.

We have four days left.

The Second Day

After a restless night, and a morning focused on yoga, apricots, and swimming in the lake, I ring Ulrich's doorbell again at 2 p.m. sharp. Although I have a key, I don't want to just burst into his apartment as usual. I now feel more like a guest than a caregiver. This time his housekeeper, who for each Thursday for decades has been taking care of the household chores and sumptuous breakfasts, complete with fresh rolls, opens the door for me.

We briefly embrace. "Not in a good mood today," she says sorrowfully in her broken German, indicating towards the dining room. "Nothing right! Clothes! Breakfast! All wrong!" Yes, I know that one, I think. And not only from him. Sometimes I feel the same way in challenging life situations.

She grabs her bag in a hurry, preparing to head off to her second housekeeping job. We say goodbye with a hug, and I peek around the corner at Ulrich. "Oh," he exclaims, "Carola, she threw away the roses! Can you imagine!" "Which roses?" "These!" He points to the empty space in the middle of the table, "the ones that were here on my table. They were a little wilted, so she just threw them away. I don't understand. My roses! My roses!"

With a heavy heart, I watch Ulrich grieve for his wilted roses, for how they ended up in the trash. Without his consent and before their time. "Ulrich, I'll go down and bring them back up!" I offer, "they've only been out there a few minutes." "No," he hollers, "no, don't!" Everything seems wrong again. There's nothing to do. Silently and full of helpless love, I stand by him, witnessing how he wrestles with his fate over the wilted roses. It's the hardest thing, not to interfere.

Nevertheless, I plan to bring him a bouquet of bright red roses tomorrow, and I'm sure that none of the three of us who work in his household will ever lay a hand on Ulrich's flowers again.

They're allowed to bloom, wilt, and fade away. Only Ulrich gets to decide when it's over. And not only with his roses.

"Would you like to take a walk around the Branitzer?" "Yeah, great!" Ulrich calls and storms off. Step by step we descend the stairs, me facing him sideways and with full focus—like a lioness ready to pounce if he threatens to topple over. That this man nearly died twice four months ago is almost unimaginable. We grab his wheelchair and I push him across the street to the square and its circular path surrounded by fading chestnut trees.

After a few meters, a call from the wheelchair commands me: "Stop! Now I want to walk! I'll push you!" We're a well-rehearsed team when it comes to changing drivers, and so now I let Ulrich push me, as he often does. The wheels bump over the small pebbles below me on the path and I have enough time to extensively study the tops of two chestnut trees and the cloudy sky between them. It's a good ten meters before Ulrich announces, "So, now, that's enough." Another changeover. And so it goes for one, two, rounds of the square.

Back in the apartment, I set the coffee table while Ulrich dozes in his chair. Silently we sip our coffee, share pieces of cake. I enjoy the quiet. "I'm sorry, I'm only concerned with myself nowadays," Ulrich suddenly sighs, deeply unsatisfied with himself after having been so curious about my life for the past two years. Indeed, he, who never showed any interest in gardening, used to enquire almost daily about my balcony and the little flower bed in front of it and everything I had sown. He, who reads everything except fiction, had wanted to be kept abreast of how I was getting on with my own novel.

Over the past two years I tried again and again to share with him the journeys and big decisions of my life. He used to just ruffle his hair. "I don't understand you, Carola. I just don't understand you." As much as that hurt me, I was touched by how much he cared and how much effort he put into it. Then one evening last

November, my phone rang. "Carola, it's Ulrich! I've just been thinking about you. I understand you, Carola! I finally understand you now!" He sounded happy, exuberant, liberated! At first I sat bolt upright on my sofa in shock, until Ulrich told me about my life in his words. I began to cry with relief and joy. From one moment to the next, I'd felt so completely understood and accepted by him in, and with, my life and the choices I'd made. It was in these moments, I tell Ulrich, that he'd fully grown to become the father of my heart.

"Yes, I remember," nods Ulrich with a big smile, "there's just one thing I still don't understand." "What do you mean?" I demand, irritated. "I don't understand why you don't have a male companion!" Bam! That stings. But to be honest, I don't either, and all at once, I'm certain that this, too, will soon change.

However, now that he's sitting next to me so dissatisfied with himself, all I can feel is immeasurable gratitude. "You've done so much for me, Ulrich! Alone this March, just a few months ago." At his questioning look, I remind him of the story. I'd been down with the flu for a few days at home and had turned my cell phone off. The first day after I was feeling better again, a text message came in from my Canadian neighbor. "An elderly gentleman is looking for you." Confused, I'd opened my door, and there was someone standing, trembling, in front of it. Ulrich. He'd looked terribly pale, and so frail after eight weeks in hospital. He'd barely been able to hold himself upright on his crutch.

"Ulrich?" I'd exclaimed in horror, "what on earth are YOU doing here??? How did you get here?" "Carola! Oh God, I was so worried about you!" "But why?" "Why don't you answer your phone? We usually talk every day! I was so worried that something had happened to you!" "Not every day, Ulrich, but almost every day," I'd managed to say in my defense, deeply shaken, and led him by the arm straight to my sofa. After a glass of water, he'd calmed down enough to tell me that he'd taken a cab to my place. Speechless, I'd sat next to him and stroked his trembling hand. That he'd even gone down the stairs and onto the street in his condition. It doesn't bear thinking about! Ulrich sighs, "Yes, I was really worried about you!" Tears are streaming down my face. "Thank you, Ulrich. Thank you so much!"

We go back to sipping our coffee. Ulrich chokes. "My strength is dwindling by the day," he coughs, looking at me in a searching, even questioning way, as if he's waiting for my confirmation. I say nothing. For what I see from the outside is a man who, for two months, has been consistently growing stronger and more independent. Confused, he looks at me. It's precisely this confusion that makes me wonder. Does he doubt himself?

I remember how he turned to me several times over the past few months. "I can't make up my mind," he'd told me desperately, "I'm conflicted." I wish I could've asked him then what it was about, but I was too close, too attached to him. "It's spiritual," Ulrich had added gloomily at the time. I'd offered, unsuccessfully, to find someone who could maybe help him. In fact, even now I'm still too involved, too biased, to support him in his self-exploration. I can only be there and listen when he wants to speak. Maybe in the process he can hear, and understand, himself.

Ulrich sleeps in his armchair until evening. I'd already noticed yesterday that the TV was standing abandoned in the corner. No news every few hours, no documentaries about history, mythology, archeology—and no more nature films. Even the newspapers from the past few days lie untouched on the table. "How are you?" I ask when he comes to again. "Pretty good. I just slept." "How about the news?" I suggest, glancing at the clock. "Oh," he says, shaking his head and rolling his eyes, "no, it's always the same nonsense anyway!"

"War!" grumbles Ulrich, "always war! They have no idea what they're talking about. You know, I was a radio operator in charge of navigating a supply ship off the coast of Norway during the war. I remember standing on deck. It was pitch black. An incredible starry sky! Auroras drifting silently and peacefully across it. In the middle of it all, I heard torpedoes hissing through the water. A hundred meters away from us a ship suddenly exploded. Then another one. Just went up. A sea of flames." Ulrich's upset voice makes me reach for his hand. He pulls it away and holds both hands in front of his face, "I just thought, *My God, the people... All these people.*"

I try to imagine it. Already with the first images that appear, a tremendous flood rises in my eyes, runs silently down my cheeks. The tears burn thick and hot on my face. Why? I wasn't there. Or are they also Ulrich's tears, which he, frozen with horror in the icy cold, could not cry at the time? He puts his hand on mine now and strokes it, comforting me through the abyss of humanity and maybe also himself a little bit, until I stop crying. Shaking his head, he says, "Those who still call for war today have never been in one. They don't know what war is."

For a long while, we sit together in silence. Noticeably relieved. The air feels cleared. At some point, we start mucking around. Giggling. Is it the tablecloth that I get caught on and almost tear off the table when I try to stand up? Nothing is too silly to make us laugh. Not because we have to laugh away any heaviness; on the contrary, because we've opened up a space where we can, yes want to, laugh again. Ulrich is gasping for breath. I'm holding my sides. "I can't anymore... stop...!" And that fires off the next burst of giggles in him.

The evening sun has long since passed the windows. Dusk is gathering around us. I switch on the light. Ulrich points to the chandelier above the table. "Notice anything?" he asks, looking mischievous. I look closely. I have to admit I know little about crystal chandeliers. "It must be worth a lot?" I try hesitantly. He points to a detail. "There! Those grapes there!

They're not originals!" I notice for the first time the numerous bunches of grapes that are hanging down from all sides of the chandelier, only I don't see any difference with these from the rest. I shrug my shoulders.

Ulrich grins. "I tore off the original grapes when I was a boy, one by one, and threw them out the window. They shattered into a thousand pieces. Such a wonderful racket it created!" I stare at him, aghast. "You did... what...?" "Got into a lot of trouble, of course..." he giggles. "With you," I splutter, "I really would've liked to play with you!" "Yes, yes... of course only then, when I inherited the chandelier from my mother, I had to have the missing parts reproduced. It was pretty expensive." We're bending over laughing. When we've finally calmed down, I peer up at the chandelier once again, and another burst of laughter shakes us.

Around 10 p.m., I help Ulrich into bed, tucking him in, and go through the night 'check' with him. With my hand on my heart and "Lots of love, Ulrich!" I bid him goodnight. Again he lies there so innocently, he too with his hand on his chest, like a little boy, fixing me with his gaze and smiling.

Deep in thought, I cycle home through the summer night. What rich facets a life holds—even and especially in these last hours.

We have three days left.

The Third Day

Friday, July 15, 2022

---

*O*ur 2 p.m. meeting today begins with a surprise: beautiful fresh red roses arranged in the middle of the table. I've no idea who brought them. "Oh, so beautiful!" I rejoice and must confess that I'd forgotten my own intention to bring some.

With the roses blooming in front of us, we enjoy a late lunch together. Ulrich is well rested and in a good mood, relieved that his nightmares from the past weeks—about people he doesn't know celebrating parties in his apartment and about greenish, featureless entities on the Branitzer Square—have suddenly ceased.

After our walk around the Branitzer and a nap, we come together for our late afternoon coffee. No sooner am I sitting next to Ulrich than I start assembling arguments convincing him to drop his plans for Monday, or at least to postpone them. My head can think of nothing else, absolutely nothing. It's hurting, cramping on the left side under my rib cage, where my heart is. It's getting worse and worse. This isn't going anywhere. How do I get out of this?

Spontaneously, in the middle of our sparring match, I snatch my cell phone from my bag. "Wait a minute!" I tell him and write myself a text message. Without quite understanding how this is going to help me, I press send. Our heated conversation instantly picks up again, dragging me helplessly along with it. A raging vortex into strangeness, senselessness, joylessness. We're interrupted by a melodious ping a few moments later. Irritated, I look at my cell and read something on it that chokes my throat, stifling any further arguments I might have:

"Love," it reads. "Believe in love! Remember love!"

Completely taken by surprise, I read this message from myself. Ulrich also looks irritated, having probably already prepared his next response to my objections. It becomes very quiet between us. I look into Ulrich's eyes, recognizing him again, the father of my heart, instead of someone I want to dissuade from doing something. My throat expands a little. Enough to take a deep breath. "Ulrich, I have to tell you something!" I say, ending our fight.

"Yes, well... where should I start," I say, looking at the table top, which is blurring before my eyes, turning into something I'm seeing for the first time. Without knowing from where they come, and in no conscious order, words start pouring out of me. It just happens on its own. I tell Ulrich how I've fought and rejected people and opportunities all my life because I thought I knew better, and how this has often blocked my path, or made it more difficult. How I've always planned everything in my head, and how it always turns out differently. And how happy I am about this now. How happy I am to be here right now, in this moment. I tell him how twice in my life I've so stubbornly run against a wall with head-long enthusiasm that I ended up in burnout.

How I crushed myself and my feelings with the merry-go-round in my head.

I tell him about the many people I know who've had or are going through a similar experience, especially the younger people I meet who are questioning this brain-centered, intellectual way of life, and are trying out something completely new for themselves. I tell him about the energy of the heart, its electric, magnetic field, which is measurably a thousand times stronger than that of our brain, and how this energy spreads throughout the world. Whether we want it to or not. Whether we believe it or not. That the energy of the heart is so infinitely more powerful than anything we construct in our heads.

I talk about how everything is, first and foremost, energy. Simultaneously particles and waves. How every particle vibrates. Electromagnetic fields generated within us and around us—all the way to the other side of the globe and beyond. I'm talking about quantum physics. Words tumble out of me, seemingly jumbled together, unplanned, linking the essence of everything I've ever lived, experienced, heard, and read. Somewhere in me I believe—no, I know—that what I'm saying touches something in Ulrich, who is widely read in the natural sciences, astronomy and cosmology, in religions, philosophy, mythology, and past civilizations.

In the middle of my outburst, I suddenly ask myself who I'm actually telling all this to. The room? The table? Ulrich? Perhaps above all, myself? Because at some point I'm also talking about the primal fundamental principle that Ulrich has repeatedly referred to over the years we've known each other, and with which he found profound and coherent resonance in me: the principle of self-responsibility.

I talk for what feels like an eternity, absorbed in the table and without looking at Ulrich, until I notice how quiet he is. Is he still there? Perhaps he's fallen asleep under my torrent of words? Looking up, I'm amazed to see him staring at the center of the table as well. Straight ahead, as if I weren't there. He looks terribly pale, shaken even. *Oh no*, I think, *this doesn't interest him at all, and I've bored him stupid.*

He blinks at me out of small, weary eyes. "I want to rest now." "Oh... yes... Sorry... Of course!" Concerned because he appears more fragile than ever, I lead him to his armchair, gently tucking him in. Before my eyes, he falls into a deep sleep. As quietly as I can, I tip-toe out of the room, unsure of whether Ulrich will ever wake up again.

What on earth was that? What was going through my head? Completely confused, I try to put things in order, at least on the outside. I wash dishes and put them away. Every now and then I sneak a peek at Ulrich, who's in a deep sleep. After an hour, I suddenly see him blink. "Ulrich?" I whisper. "Come here!" he says softly. Unsure, I approach. He takes my hand. "Thank you for talking to me." Taken by surprise, I sit down close to him on the floor without letting go of his hand. Is he serious? We look at each other for a long, long time. His eyes are incredibly soft, letting me all the way in. Then he begins to speak.

"Thank you," he says, serious and gentle at the same time, "thank you for this conversation, Carola. I only ever have conversations like this with you." I can hardly believe it. Tears are streaming down my face. Something I've told him has touched him. I realize he can't say more at the moment. Or that he doesn't want to. So we just sit together, holding eye contact without blinking. Wide open. Soft. Free. As the evening sun shines into the room, leisurely wandering past the bookshelves to the writing desk, a mighty love gently flows between us.

"Father of my Heart!"
"Daughter of my Heart!"

I bend over into him and for a long while we hold each other.

When the sun moves through the branches of the tree outside, I ask, "Shall we watch the evening coming in, Ulrich?" His whole being beams one solid yes, nested in his wide, peaceful smile.

Sitting together at the window, we remain silent for a long time. "Everything is energy!" I finally say, filled with wonder, as if to myself. "The chairs we sit on. That sofa over there. The sun's rays on your arm. Basically, everything is nothing but energy." Ulrich nods thoughtfully, recalling essays, cosmic and physical ways of looking at life, things he's seen and read on his many travels. Whatever we say cross-fertilizes our knowledge and our experiences. The fighting is over. Perhaps it's now, in these moments, that we create the deepest, most intimate connection between us as father and daughter.

After that, everything is like new. Serene. Calm. Smooth. Peaceful. Our dinner together. Ulrich's evening hygiene routine, which I help him with. It's early, and yet he wants to go to sleep. Lying in bed, snuggled up to his chin under his blanket, he looks at me; I burst with deep unity and infinite love. Today we skip the evening check to see if everything is in the right place for the night.

Instead, our ritual takes on a whole new dimension. I put my hand on my heart. "Ulrich, dear one! Lots and lots and lots of love!" In the glow of the bedside lamp, Ulrich's face lights up like the sun in the middle of the day as he too places his hand on his heart and I cover his with mine. With his eyes closed, he's nodding. Nodding and nodding. When I switch off the lamp, the room remains bright.

As quietly as I can, I sneak out. Contrary to my usual habits, I leave the dishes from the evening on the dining room table. On my way home I feel that everything is good, whatever that may mean. And this:

We have two days left.

The Fourth Day

Today, I make it a point to wait until quarter past two to ring Ulrich's doorbell. I'm hoping that his nurse, whom I actually like a lot, will have already left by then, taking with her her intense emotional outbursts over Ulrich's decision. I don't want my inner peace disturbed anymore.

However, I'm not late enough—she opens the door. We hug each other, she briefly reports on the mood and practical details for the handover, and then starts crying. "I don't understand it. Ulrich wants to die on Monday, but every morning he keeps doing his gymnastics and autogenic training. I can't believe it. Why does he do that? He wants to die. I can't put it together."

Confused, I look at her. Do I understand him? It dawns on me that he probably just wants to feel as good as possible, that it's important to him to live his everyday life until his last breath; to savor all that brings him joy and strength to get through the day. The few things that remain from his rich life that he can still do for himself without any help. That's how he lives, handing himself completely over to life, just as he always has. Until the end. He wants to die in life.

I can't explain this to her. I think it's because in truth her question isn't a question at all, but rather a frantic search for arguments and ways to dissuade him from his plans on Monday; to keep him with her at least until the fall. "Stay until the end of summer!" she's been begging him. I understand her so well, I myself acted like that until yesterday. Now I see how tiring such resistance is and how it already separates her from Ulrich before the time comes. I'm relieved to notice how I've gradually repositioned myself and am instead walking a path together with him.

She leaves in tears. I go to Ulrich, kissing his forehead and calling out "Hi! How are you today?" before sitting down next to him on the glazed balcony. Without answering me, he bursts out in a cheerful voice, "Yes! Yes, Carola! That's exactly how it is! Everything is energy! And then..." he laughs high spiritedly, mischievously, swinging his arms up and down lightly and happily, "... and then... then I'll buzz around you on Monday! Bzzzzzzzz...!"

His laughter rings out like bright bells. Surprised by Ulrich's inner transformation, I drink it in as if from an eternally bubbling spring. Has our conversation from yesterday stayed with him? "Yes!" I reply with a relieved laugh, "yes! Yes! Exactly like that, dear Ulrich! Bzzzzzzzz..." Our arms become wings sailing through the air, and we embrace each other giddily like two children, buzzing and whirring while the sun peeks out from behind gray summer clouds for the first time today.

Light-heartedly, Ulrich shows me his fist. "Look! Where's my thumb?" I freeze, turning nine years old again. Not because his thumb is gone, but because there was only one person in my life who played this game with me. Until they couldn't anymore. Laughing merrily, Ulrich pulls his thumb from his fist, but my expression remains deadly serious. "Why did you just do that?" I ask. "What do you mean?" "The thing with your thumb. That's what my father used to play with me. I could never get enough of it." Ulrich shrugs his shoulders. My father passed away long before Ulrich came into my life. Now Ulrich has awakened him. It almost feels as if the three of us are sitting here together now. Me with my two fathers. And it feels strangely harmonious.

When I was between nine and eleven years old, my two fathers were geographically separated by nothing more than a peninsula. The Talamanka, my parents' sailing boat on which we spent our summers, was tethered to a buoy in the Scharfe Lanke lake, just one bay away from the lake where Ulrich's sailing boat, the Pegasus, was moored. I wonder if we ever sailed past each other. Would we have recognized each other?

Ulrich leaves me to my thoughts, preferring instead to study the chestnut tree in front of us at length. There's nothing to say. Later, it draws us down to the Branitzer, from bench to bench. Afterwards, as we sit having our afternoon coffee, Ulrich points to the adjoining living room. "Just two more days and then I'm dead," he says, thoughtfully, between two cookies. "Well, and if someone calls next week, then you just say *Ulrich has died.* It's simple." My jaw drops. It's simple? Is that how he sees the time after his passing here? That we'll all continue to keep ourselves busy in his apartment, without him, taking calls, as though he's just left to travel for a while?

He goes one better. "Tomorrow evening we'll move the couch a little away from the wall and then I'll lie on it on Monday when the doctor comes. And then we'll hold the funeral!" I snort coffee across the table in a high arc. "No," I blurt out furiously between coughing fits. "No, my dear Ulrich, WE won't be doing anything more together. YOU will have died and WE will hold the funeral alone, namely those of us who are still alive!" Now it's Ulrich's turn to pause in shock, then confess with a giggle, "Oh baloney! I won't be there anymore!" Unable to contain himself, he chuckles.

"Do you feel like going down for a walk?" Ulrich thinks for a moment and confesses, "Unfortunately, I don't have the strength today. But let's do a few rounds up here!" I push the walker towards him and wait until he's stable. He immediately takes off, counterclockwise around the long eight-seater dining table, with me close at his heels, arms wide open but without touching him, like a cat ready to pounce at any moment if he, bent forward a little, threatens to stagger out of the maximum swing range of his body axis. A fine balancing act, but we're a well-rehearsed team. Sometimes all it takes is a light tap on his spine and he straightens up enough to regain his own balance. Like a sailing ship in a storm. Still, as always, I'm relieved when he declares the workout over and sits down again.

Ulrich sleeps the afternoon hours away in his armchair. After we've eaten dinner, he asks, "Why? But why? Why didn't I get out?" Prisoner of war Ulrich, at the end of World War II, crammed in among so many others in train wagons with open doors, on his way from Norway to a prison camp somewhere in France. "So many got off. In the middle of nowhere, our train just stopped. Not a guard for miles. On the tracks opposite, there was a passenger train waiting, heading for Berlin. *Come*, the people shouted, *come, get off! Come over to us!* So many jumped off, went over to the train to Berlin. And me? Why didn't I get off?" He asks himself the question, but points it in my direction.

His gaze looks through me, far, far back to where the unresolved questions of his life are waiting for him. I have no answer, and any attempt at consolation would be nothing but garrulous platitudes. Infinitely touched by his earnest, even reproachful self-questioning, I simply remain open and silent next to him. After a while he looks me directly in the eyes. "Yes, that's it, Carola, that's exactly what war and the military do to people. You forget to think for yourself. I had to relearn that."

"What was it like back then? You were only eight years old when Hitler came to power. Do you remember that time? The first Hitler salute at school or anything like that?" "Well," says Ulrich, thinking, "it kind of happened gradually. I remember my time at the boarding school. Our gym teacher gathered us together to go to the house of a Jewish family in the village and smash their windows with rocks." I gulp. "The gym teacher? How old were you then?" "Ten or eleven I must've been. Anyway, I asked him why we should break the windows. The people who lived there were nice, weren't they?" "Yes, and then?" Ulrich looks at me in irritation. "Well, the windows stayed intact, of course." Yes, of course. What else?

"Were you in the Hitler Youth?" Ulrich shakes his head. "I had to report to the police station at the Charlottenburg Palace in the evening and spend the night there instead. After a few nights," he laughs, "they'd had enough of me and I could go home again!"

"And how did you end up in the marines during the war?" "One day, men from the secret police came to our classroom. They asked which of us could count and write well. I raised my hand and said that I could. Well, and then they took me to training with some other boys." "How old were you? Fourteen? Fifteen?" Ulrich shrugs his shoulders.

Briefly, I consider asking him why he went. Why he didn't refuse. However, I remember that at a young age he was sent to boarding school with his sister, and a short time after that he was separated from her when she was transferred to a girls' school 'for affluent daughters'. I remember him telling me he was terribly homesick and cried at night. I also remember that Ulrich's father died when he was just three years old. This teenage Ulrich had had no real support in life. Left on his own far too early. Anger is boiling up inside me. Yes, the boys were easy prey there in the boarding school, isolated from their families. Only a few could go home to the neighboring villages in the evenings. I fume. I want to nail these men with their uniforms to the wall. *Look me in the eyes! What the hell were you thinking?* I want to shout at them.

"The other boys who didn't report so quickly were sent to the Russian front. Cannon fodder..." Ulrich continues, saddened. "I was really lucky, assigned as a radio operator on a supply ship up in the Nordic waters off Norway." "I remember. You told me about that yesterday. About the ships exploding." Ulrich nods silently.

"And how did you end up a prisoner of war? And when?" I want to know. Ulrich falters, can't put the details together anymore, becomes quite desperate. "My God, it's all mixed up," he pulls at his sparse hair. I can hardly bear to see him suffering like this.

"Will you tell me again how you escaped captivity in southern France?" I ask him. "I think the story is so incredible. Full of miracles!" "Okay. The war was actually over. French soldiers had put me up with some other prisoners in a village. The farmer's wife where I was being held insulted and disparaged me in the worst possible way. It was terrible. After a few weeks, I'd learned enough French to hit back at her the next time she verbally attacked me. From then on, she left me alone."

I grin. Yes, as I know from experience, being scolded by Ulrich is extremely unpleasant. "We were treated badly, freezing and starving, and living in filth. The first time I escaped was at night with a fellow prisoner. After just a few kilometers, French soldiers approached us. My buddy didn't jump into the ditch fast enough. They caught us. *Ulrich, you have to escape on your own*, I told myself at the time." He stares at me urgently with a 'remember that' look.

"I prepared my second escape well. I needed a compass, so I searched for an aluminum nail in a barn, and traded cigarettes for a sewing needle with another prisoner. I made a small dent right in the center of the needle so it could swing freely on the tip of the nail." I whistle through my teeth. "Ah, aluminum! I see. The carrier of the magnetic needle can't be magnetic, otherwise it deflects the pointer. But how did you get it to line up?" "I found a rusty bicycle with lamps. I took out the battery, removed the magnet, and magnetized the needle with it." "Gee, Ulrich! How inventive you are!" "If you knew how great my distress was..." "But the magnetic needle had to rest exactly on the tip of the nail in such a way that it wouldn't tilt, but could swing freely. How did you manage that?" Ulrich laughs. "Patience!" I almost have to laugh in the middle of his painful recollection. There's just something deeply absurd to me about the word 'patience' coming out of Ulrich's mouth. "I just kept working on it. When the compass was finished, I traded my saved cigarette rations for a drawing of a map by a fellow prisoner. At the next opportunity, I escaped again. I only ever moved at night. During the day, I hid in the forest and slept under bushes."

"What did you survive on?" "Well, from the bread in my little bag. I'd saved that from my daily rations and roasted it in the oven to preserve it." I try to imagine all this. "Did you steal food, too?" Ulrich laughs. "No, that was too dangerous. But after a few days, my feet were so sore in my soaking wet boots that I stole a bicycle from a village. And guess what—some kids saw me and told the mayor! He had me arrested immediately." I'm holding my breath. "The village magistrate put me in jail for a week as punishment. But," Ulrich laughs, "I was the only prisoner! And the prison guard's wife liked me. She cooked for me and brought a thick down bed to my cell. *Le pauvre prisonnier!* she always called out when she saw me. The woman nursed me back to health. After a week, I asked for my sentence to be extended to a month so I could recover properly. But the judge only gave me an extra week." "Unbelievable..." I murmur.

"Then I went off again. When it was dark, I walked into the small towns and looked into the lighted windows. Where there were young people, just like me, I dared to knock and ask for food." "So you never knew if they would betray you?" I ask, stunned by his courage. "No, but what else could I do? In Basel, a woman invited me to stay for a few days. I confided to her that I wanted to cross the border but had no papers. She said she could help me. The next night she went with me to the Swiss-German border, where her friend, the Basel chief of police himself, was waiting for us. He helped me get past the checkpoint into Germany without a passport." "I don't believe it," I cheer, "you were incredibly lucky!"

Ulrich's voice cracks. "My God, and then the sandwiches!" he laughs and shakes his head as if amused by an old film, "the twenty-three sandwiches!" "Yes, what was it again? The woman made them for you, right? But why twenty-three?" "Well, she'd heard that the people crossing the borders into Germany were first held for a few days while their personal details were checked. There'd be a lot of men locked in a room and they'd all be hungry. *Share your sandwiches with them, and they'll be kind to you!* she told me." "And—was she right?" "Yes, she was! After a few days I carried on. In a village, I knocked on doors again at night. Again a woman gave me shelter. She even gave me money for a train ticket to Berlin. And a suit! It was her son's. I think he was killed in the war." I could cry with horror and joy.

"And then?" I bathe in the flow of his narrative, which—although I'm familiar with the broad outlines of it—always presents new cliffhangers, sucking me into new whirlpools. Into his energy, his pure life, unpredictable like a female dog in heat. "I took the next train to Berlin and found myself standing before my mother at her door. Months before, she'd asked a fortune teller about my fate. She'd been told I was alive and on my way home. So my mother wasn't particularly surprised—although she was blown away by the fact I stood before her well-fed and elegant in a black suit! Of course, I told her the whole escape story. At the end she just laughed. *Uli, you always had too much imagination...!*" "Your mother didn't believe you?" Ulrich shrugs. "I'm not sure..." "Anyway, someone powerful was definitely watching over you!" I say, both moved and grateful, "luck stood by you faithfully and kindly." "Yes! And all the people who helped me. I visited one of the women later with my family..."

We sit together speechless for a while, letting the many memories fade away. Ulrich suddenly looks so incredibly tired.

It's now well past 11 p.m. In reverent silence, I help him into bed. With my hand I rub vigorous circles on his bedspread-covered chest. "Dear Ulrich! Lots of love!" Ulrich smiles, looking blissful. The man from a moment ago, exhausted from his escape, now looks at me again like a little boy from shining eyes. We do the 'equipment check', I complete it with a cup of water, kiss Ulrich on the forehead, and am happy to know he's safe for the night.

On the bike ride home, it occurs to me that I don't have any cash. After taking a two kilometer detour to an ATM machine, it informs me that it's unfortunately out of order today, but points out that I can withdraw money at most Shell gas stations. I feel incredibly discouraged having cycled the two kilometers for nothing. I'm so exhausted and drained from the day.

On the opposite side of the street, I spot a gas station. Shell. I wonder if they...? I try to convince myself that I don't need any money until tomorrow. And I almost, almost give up—until Ulrich comes to mind. His courage to traverse more than a thousand kilometers of unknown terrain, simply because he'd wanted to get home. I have to laugh out loud at myself. Here I am, a lunatic of civilization, and I don't dare to try my luck at the gas station across the street? And behold: The young man at the checkout smiles at me. "How much do you want?"

I promise myself that I'll remember this if I ever lose heart again. And then there's tomorrow.

We have one whole day left.

The Fifth Day

*I*t's finally dawned, our fifth and last day together. By now I'm so used to our new way of spending afternoons and evenings with each other that I can hardly imagine having to say goodbye to it tomorrow. Let alone to Ulrich.

Carefully, I pack a few small items for dinner in my basket. My gaze falls on the bright pink, blooming oleander in the garden. As if from nowhere, it appeared there weeks ago, planted in an antique-looking plastic pot. Since it remained ownerless in spite of my note, I adopted it. Without understanding what I would need it for today, I clamp it under my arm, which is surprisingly easy due to the pot's material, and set off to see Ulrich shortly before 1 p.m. This time by car, because I'm hoping we'll drive to the café of his sailing club on this last, beautiful summer afternoon. To drink coffee there one more time.

No sooner have I unlocked Ulrich's apartment door than he greets me with an upset "Carola, do you know where the egg cooker is? I've already looked everywhere. I can't find it. Do you know where it is? It was always next to the microwave." I'm so perplexed that I forget to laugh, and ask back, seriously, "What egg cooker? I've never seen one standing there." "Yes you have," he insists, "the egg cooker has always been there. Where did it go? I don't get it. Who would take something like that?" Instead of getting into a discussion about potential egg-cooker thieves, I go into the kitchen and thoroughly search all the cupboards.

I hear Ulrich out on his glazed balcony on the phone, now including his favorite nurse in the egg cooker hunt. As I pull on a cable at the very back of the kitchen cupboard, directly under the microwave, a dusty thing comes towards me and I can hardly contain my laughter. With the trophy in my hands, I position myself directly in front of an astonished Ulrich.

"Look what I've got here!" I splutter. "Oh, there it is!" he replies with relief, only to burst out laughing right after. "No! No!" he chortles, ruffling his sparse white hair, "such nonsense! I'm going to die tomorrow! What do I need an egg cooker for!" He can't contain himself any longer, and my stomach starts to hurt from laughing too. Again and again I shake Ulrich's arm to make myself heard between bursts of laughter. "Ulrich! Ulrich!—Now listen to me—Ulrich! Do you know…" I giggle, "do you know what's the best part, Ulrich? Do you know what I brought for tonight? Eggs! But for fried eggs!" "Fried eggs?" Again we splutter.

Just as we're standing in the doorway finally ready to go to the sailing club, Ulrich's housekeeper approaches us. We hug each other warmly. I like her a lot; she showed me unconditional warmth during the months I lived with Ulrich, touchingly leaving me a pile of freshly washed and lovingly ironed underwear on my bed each week. Now she's come to say goodbye to Ulrich. My stomach knots again. For more than thirty years, she's taken care of his household once a week, preparing breakfast for him with fresh rolls and treating him with home-cooked food from her Polish repertoire. We go back into the apartment.

One look at Ulrich and I notice that he's uncomfortable with the situation as she sits down next to him and wants to start a conversation. Both seem immensely helpless with each other. In truth, it feels like there's little to say. But it's not my concern, and so I retreat into the kitchen to wash the dishes. Everywhere there's this awareness of 'the last time'. With the clean dishes in front of me and an exasperated "Puuuuh..." I wait at the sink, listening for the sounds of a farewell, footsteps, a closing door. The minute hand on the large kitchen clock is eating up our precious time.

I take advantage of the moment and look in Ulrich's bedroom to check if everything's ready for the night. On the wall opposite his bed I notice the piles of yellowed paper next to files and overflowing plastic bags. Horrified, I realize that Ulrich has already cleared out his desk. My God, he thinks of everything indeed.

Still no sign of a farewell to be seen from the

living room. Now my patience explodes. Rarely has it been as cliché as it is now—but every minute of Ulrich's last afternoon in life counts. Resolutely, I march back to the two of them, catching Ulrich's relieved, pleading-for-help look. "We were just about to go to the sailing club for coffee when you came!" I explain to his housekeeper. She immediately stands up, and he with her. Their goodbye is short, almost brusque. Then I escort her out and say goodbye too, waving as she goes down the stairs and looks around once more, blowing me a kiss. We both know that we'll meet again at the funeral.

I don't even get a chance to close the apartment door because Ulrich is already at the threshold ready to break out. "Wait!" I just manage to stop him from going down the stairs alone. Quickly, I grab his sun hat and jacket and hold the walking stick out to him with questioning eyes. "Oh yes!" he grins. I grin back. We know each other!

In the garden café, I prepare a chair for Ulrich with extra cushions. From there he has a direct view of the boats and the lake. I sit down close to him. The afternoon sun shimmers through the trees, softening Ulrich's face, with his mouth stretched wide as if in a permanent smile. I have no idea what's going on behind it. I sit with him, just letting him be. Is he still asking himself whether tomorrow is the right time for him? Is there even a right time? And whether it would be better for him to wait until his life comes to a natural end?

A woman approaches our table. I don't know her, but she obviously knows Ulrich. "Hello Mr. B.!" she brightly calls, "how are you?" Ulrich looks at her with interest and a little confusion. "Pretty good!" I'm floored at how he can say that so easily and still want to die tomorrow. She smiles at him with sympathy. "My mother's fine, too! She's a hundred now and lives in a nursing home. She can still walk quite well, and she likes it there!" I'm eagerly waiting for Ulrich's reaction, as this woman unwittingly shows him an alternative, a possible future for him too, so shortly before the gates close. "I don't want to live to be a hundred," he replies in a firm voice, shaking his head vigorously. It becomes quiet, so quiet between the two of them. The balmy summer wind blows speechlessly into all of our faces. "All the best, Mr. B.!" she says. "For you too!" smiles Ulrich.

We sit together in silence, empty cake plates in front of us. Every now and then I squeeze Ulrich's hand. There's simply nothing to say. Suddenly he urges, "We have to go home and prepare everything for tomorrow." Prepare? I nod, feeling nauseous.

Armed with a twenty Euro bill from Ulrich, I go to the counter to pay. One last time that he's treating me. "You're invited," he would always laugh mischievously in his best Berlin manner, "not expected to pay!" As I hand over his money, I wonder why I didn't offer to pay for HIM? Wouldn't that be more appropriate? But I'm craving a little fatherly nourishment from him, especially in these last hours.

Back at the table, I offer him my right arm. Hooked in it and leaning on his cane on the other side, he moves laboriously along the narrow gravel path that separates the terrace from the lawn where we met sixteen years ago. Where his boat, the Pegasus, has been moored for years now under new ownership. When I ask him if he wants to go to the Pegasus one last time, he surprises me. "No," he says, without a moment's hesitation. As much as he sways on my arm, he seems clear and firm in his decision.

I help him into the car, buckle him up, realizing it's the last time. No more having coffee together at his sailing club. And this car ride is also our—and above all his—last. Leisurely, I drive north along the avenue towards his apartment. I go well below the speed limit of thirty kilometers an hour to enable us, and especially him, to say goodbye to this route which has been part of his everyday sailing life for more than half a decade. It's a farewell without words.

We both know it's the last time. We travel along Reichs Street, left onto Platanen Boulevard, and another left onto Chestnut Boulevard, parking directly in front of his house where I urge him to wait a last time before getting out of the car until I can meet him at the passenger door. Once again he climbs the stairs to his mighty front door. Every step costs him the strength he's worked so hard to regain over the last few months. I admire him more than I can say.

For the last time, he pulls out his keys and unlocks his front door. Without taking off his jacket, he storms straight into the living room, dangerously unsteady on his feet after the exertion of climbing the stairs, and begins to instruct me. "Move the table a little away from the sofa!" I notice that he doesn't preface his request with a friendly "Oh, please..." as usual. His tone is also unusually urgent, as if we were on a ship and he, the skipper, senses imminent danger. "Now move the sofa away from the wall!" I don't like this commanding tone, and yet I follow it without resistance. "A bit more!" Despite the demands, there's something tremendously sacred in this act of being asked to prepare his deathbed.

He makes me move the table a little to the left, a little to the right, and then even further away from the sofa, a few more times. Something in me wishes this will never end, that I can go on moving the furniture a few centimeters here and there for decades to come, when Ulrich suddenly announces: "It's good now. On Monday I'll lie down there on the sofa." My eyes open wide. The banality of his words, his voice, which was just moments ago so dignified, shocks me. Appalled, I look first at him as he sinks, noticeably relieved, into his TV chair and leans back; then I take in the final version of this still life composed of sofa and table. I realize that from now on I will never sit there again.

While Ulrich is napping, and since the sofa is no longer an option for my resting place, I retreat to the music room, running a finger over the slightly dusty grand piano, and searching for a connection to my mother, who on a Christmas Eve a few years ago played the notes to 'Oh, come, little children...' on this piano. Oh, if I could come to you now, Mom, because having to endure all this alone is really challenging.

Suddenly I remember the oleander that's still at the bottom of the stairs by the front door. At least I hope so. I sneak down and carry the giant pot up, happy and once again amazed at how it just appeared in the garden and is so easy to carry. As if it was just waiting for its purpose. Which I discern now is to keep watch, a symbol of life, at the head end of the sofa on which Ulrich will die tomorrow. Underneath I place a rose quartz, a piece of wood, matches, and a bowl of water; on the table I lay a candle, which I'll light tomorrow. With this, the place is prepared for me as well. When Ulrich slowly regains consciousness and quietly contemplates the scene, he smiles a satisfied, almost happy yes and nods off again.

I'm wandering between the music room and the glazed balcony when the phone rings. Through the open door, I hear Ulrich's voice, have a funny feeling, and go over to him. I just catch him saying "See you tomorrow!" Then he hangs up. I look at him questioningly. It was the doctor. About tomorrow. He'd asked Ulrich how he was feeling about it and whether he wanted to postpone. "No," Ulrich recounts to me, "no, it stays that way. As agreed." The finality in his words pulls the rug out from under me and I have to lean against the door frame.

Anger flashes through me. Ideally, I want Ulrich to give me the doctor's phone number. I want to know who this man is, how he speaks, who it is that's coming tomorrow to send the father of my heart into the after-life. How exactly will this happen? Am I even allowed to be with Ulrich? Sit with him? Hold his hand if he wants me to? This uncontrollable anger brings tears to my eyes, tears of helplessness, of being lost in the un-known. And that's what I decide to embrace: whatever and however it will be, it's okay. I don't need to know everything and certainly not the doctor's number.

"Shall we sit by the window and watch the evening come in?" I ask Ulrich. I open the window, move our two chairs into place, and help him over to his. I make myself comfortable on his right. We sit to-gether in the silence that's so familiar to us. After a while, he talks about the property across the street. Of one of the upper middle-class villas with a garden that's growing increasingly out of control—at least in Ulrich's eyes. Again he tells me the story of the garden, planted in such a way that something's always in bloom all year round. He points to the chestnuts, which have grown particularly vigorously on the south side.

"Look!" he points to the tree opposite, "look! The pigeons! There used to be so many of them here. Now there are only a few." I look at the two birds as they hang sedately onto the branches and now and then fly up with a loud flapping of their wings to land anew. "Yes, the pigeons!" I nod and admire their somewhat ponderous beauty.

Minutes pass until I hear Ulrich's urgent voice next to me: "Just look! Those pigeons there!" My brow furrows. What's that supposed to mean? Sure, he's often gotten things mixed up in the last few months, sometimes forgetting who he'd already told something to or when exactly an appointment was due. But to be honest—not that different from myself. I've never experienced anything like this with him before though. "Yes," I say distinctly, "yes, I see them, the two pigeons there in the tree!"

Ulrich stares at the birds as if mesmerized. A strange feeling of timelessness is spreading, making me light, and my head gets muddled, a bit tipsy. I feel as if I'm losing the footing beneath me. I press my feet into the parquet and hold Ulrich's hand a little tighter. Although physically present, he seems far, far away, his gaze fixed on the two birds. I sense a vastness around us, growing ever wider. Time seems to stand still. I marvel at how it's possible to feel so lost in this space and at the same time, so infinitely held and protected.

Yet again, Ulrich points to the tree opposite, suddenly, and with a powerful gesture, shouting: "Just look! The two pigeons there in the tree!" It's his voice, but he sounds as if he's speaking from far away. Almost as if something is speaking through him, as if he's just a mouthpiece for something I cannot understand.

Maybe it's the incredible vastness around us, the seriousness, the inexorable radical focus with which he directs my attention again and again to these two birds, in addition to his voice, which seems to me as if remote-controlled, trying to reach me from a great distance. A force, a clarity innocent as a child, overwhelms me, startling me so much that I have to put my hand over my eyes in disbelief, as if protecting myself. Part of me fights what I perceive. What nonsense. That's absurd. But the more I try resisting it, the clearer it becomes. Tears stream down my face, washing away my defenses and opening up something in me that I've never experienced to this extent before. An unconditional, accepting humility of life, of the wonders we cannot understand, of what's just happened, which spreads through me like warmth from an oven.

Through the two pigeons, Ulrich creates a connection between us that goes far beyond us sitting next to each other in our wooden chairs. I have no words for this. I receive it, I feel it, in every single one of my cells. Whatever it means, I accept it. Anchored in my deepest yes, I squeeze Ulrich's hand. Out of the corner of my eye, I see his mouth expand into a never-ending, luminous smile, like an inverted rainbow. Then a hint of a nod. We sit in silence for a while. He doesn't mention the pigeons again. Instead, a little later he turns to where his armchair is located in the corner. "So, now I'd like to rest for a while!"

I help him to the armchair and sit down on the floor at his feet, leaning against his legs, while he dozes. When he opens his eyes, he announces "Wait a minute!", rises swaying and, as if he might be late, storms out of the room to his bedroom without his walker. I hear him rummaging, unsure of whether to follow him in case he suddenly loses his balance. But something tells me to wait. After a few minutes he returns with something in his hand, which he holds out to me with great seriousness.

"Would you like to have this?" For as long as I've known him, he's not only carried his money under his shirt in the worn, black leather chest pouch; but also a very special pocket knife, ultra-flat and equally light, resembling a razor-sharp stamp, held between two black plastic folds and secured with a small wheel. I have to swallow hard and tears come to my eyes again.

What he wants to bequeath to me is something that's played a very, very important and special role in his life, and I feel infinitely honored. At the same time, his gift is a brutal testimony to the firmness of his resolve—tomorrow his life here will be over. I just nod and carefully take the heirloom in my hand. Ulrich shows me how to unlock it, and I practice a few times. But the real legacy he's leaving me are his wishes for my well-being and safety, interwoven with his encouragement for me to defend myself to the death if necessary.

With the knife secured in my hand, I sit leaning against Ulrich's legs again and keep looking up at him, into his eyes, with all the love that floods our last hours together. Something is working within him. Gently, he grabs my wrist and, barely palpably, feels the silver bracelet set with turquoise stones. "From Greece?" "Yes, I bought it for myself," I smile proudly and happily as I remember it. "I still have some jewelry..." Ulrich stands up abruptly and staggers towards the bedroom again. Shaking his head, he returns empty-handed. "Oh no, I already gave it all to my son for his girlfriend...!" Once again I don't know whether to laugh or cry. And it's not because of the jewelry.

Ulrich looks around the living room, searching. Past the shelves of his library with double rows of books. Not decorative, but books he's read, some of them worn out, about countries, oceans, animals and plants, about advanced civilizations from long ago, mythology, the cosmos, philosophy and travel—all of which Ulrich used to ponder for hours. Even on the tables in his apartment there were always new books filled with bookmarks and notes written in pencil.

Buddhism. The construction of the pyramids. The Living Sea by Jacques Yves Cousteau. All the things I've loved talking to him about over the past few years. What happens to all this knowledge in his head, all his insights and questions, when he dies?

He looks along his Rococo writing dresser, his eyes finally settling on something in the corner by the window. "Would you like the barometer?" I look over. It hangs beautifully, round and framed in shiny varnished wood, on the wall by the window, ready for Ulrich to read the weather each morning with a light tap. "Yes, I'd love it!" I say, touched. "Bring it here!" he prompts me.

I carefully take it off the wall. It's surprisingly heavy in my hands. "You have to replace the batteries!" he says very seriously, and looks at me. "Oh yeah? "What kind of batteries go in here?" I ask. Ulrich raises his shoulders as if clueless, while the corners of his mouth twitch. I feel observed as I turn the heavy barometer back and forth in my hands, searching for the flap behind which the batteries must be hidden. And from the weight of it, there must be a lot of the big fat ones in there. "Where are batteries supposed to go?" I ask it, perplexed. Suddenly Ulrich is cracking up and can't stop himself. I frown, looking from him to the barometer and back until I, too, burst out laughing. "Of course!" I laugh, "Of course!"

We giggle and laugh and hold our sides. When we've calmed down, Ulrich explains to me what I'd forgotten amidst all my emotions. "It works through differences in pressure." "Yes... yes... of course... I know!" I laugh, "you really got me there!" He grins, rubbing his hands together, and points to the barometer in my hand. "You can take the blood pressure monitor home with you later." I stare at him. "Blood pressure monitor?" I ask. "Blood pressure monitor?" he asks back, puzzled. And again we splutter with laughter until we're gasping for breath.

For dinner I prepare fried eggs for us the way Ulrich likes them. With every bite I feel our time together draining away. The hourglass gets emptier and can no longer be turned. Our last half hour together is beginning—Ulrich's nephew has already texted saying that he's arrived in Berlin on schedule and is on his way here as agreed.

When he rings the bell, a huge shock runs through my limbs. From now on, we'll no longer be alone. That special time—just Ulrich and I—when he says things like "I only have conversations like this with you," is now over. Admittedly, I'm also a little relieved. It had to end at some point. A farewell like this can't be delayed forever without ending up being nothing but agonizing. From now on, other people will also be here with him. With us.

Ulrich and his nephew greet each other warmly. The affection and joy the two of them have for each other fills both the room and me. The nephew settles down on the chair that I've sat on until now, and I'm happy to leave it to him. Instead, I carry the dishes into the kitchen without washing them up.

Back at the table, the two men are lost in conversation. From one second to the next, I feel completely ignored. I'm just about to say goodbye when I hear Ulrich's voice. "Bring us water!" Neither a kind request nor a question but instead a statement—no, a command. For the second time today. My shoulders tighten and I feel ice cold as I again follow strangely obediently, trotting into the kitchen and only pausing in front of the faucet. I've never experienced this Ulrich before. Where am I? Was that once the tone in this sophisticated, stuccoed-filled six-room apartment with a servants' entrance, when there had still been maids, long before Ulrich and his family moved in here?

I remember the small, frequently rung bronze bell on the table in the living room positioned to the right of Ulrich. For the last few months he always wanted to have it nearby, even when I replaced it with an indoor electronic alarm. So far the bell has amused me, even touched me. This witness of past times, which I have often weighed in the palm of my hand as if testing it, ringing it myself for fun. The tone is bright and at the same time oppressive. What if someone had come?

Now I feel really uncomfortable. I sense them, these humiliating facets of a maid's existence from long ago. Someone who unquestioningly submitted to the rulers, remaining silent, keeping her eyes, if not lowered, then at least focused on them. The existence of a woman who experiences life, her own, solely through all the rights and wrongs that shake like earthquakes in the facial expressions of those in power. So this is how it may have once been. Horror grips me. Also because of myself. I swallow, acknowledging these traits of obedience from the past that are also still in me. Even though I wear neither a white bonnet nor an apron, I say goodbye to this world by slamming two glasses onto the table for the two men, spilling water in the process:

"That was the last order! The kitchen is now closed!"

In the middle of the banter, which seconds ago completely ignored me, the two pause, looking up. With open mouths. Too stunned to even utter a word. I enjoy it. The attention. That I am standing and they are sitting. A few seconds where maids across the centuries tear off their white aprons, their bonnets, with a single phrase, a single gesture—"The kitchen is now closed." It's about time. And still, I think that Ulrich will die tomorrow. I just can't puzzle it all together.

Maybe it's easier this way. Being a little mean gives me the distance I need, the strength to keep from falling to the ground. I kiss Ulrich heartily on the forehead and try to counter the pain in my heart. It's the last evening and I'd imagined our farewell today a little differently. "Bye," I say, straining to sound cheerful, and dismiss myself for one last time before *the day,* which is now looming imminently.

As I walk down the stairs to my car, to my life, I feel myself becoming a little lighter with each step. Strangely glad to leave it all behind. The worries about the well-being of the father of my heart. I know he's in good hands now, passed over to his nephew, whom Ulrich has known since birth. While Ulrich had, as a young man, changed the diapers of his sister's little son, it was now up to the nephew to help his uncle with his hygiene in these last hours. How miraculously the circles always close.

And I know the two men will celebrate now. Catching up on family stories that happened long before my time and toasting to life. After consulting with Ulrich, the nephew has brought a bottle of the best sparkling wine for the occasion. Above all, they will toast Ulrich's life. Again and again. I'm happy for them.

Because we celebrated too, Ulrich and I. For five days. In our own way. The strangest celebration—with its ups and downs, tears, seismic laughter, hiccuping giggles and questions that gave birth to their own answers. Yes, and now suddenly everything feels so complete, so finished, that I sit for a while in the car at my front door, crying with gratitude.

In the evening, my thoughts keep drifting back to Ulrich and his nephew. It feels so good to know the two of them are together. It's late at night when I turn off my light, noticeably calm about tomorrow, although I'm still wondering whether I'll actually go there and be a witness. I'm well aware that if I cancel tomorrow morning, so close to closing time, the whole event will fall through. But that's how it is. If Ulrich exercises his free will with his decision tomorrow, I will do the same. Whatever may happen.

What lets me find the way into my night's rest, despite my not-knowing, is a powerful sense of trust that the answer will come when it's ready. At the right time.

As I drift off to sleep, an image comes to me of Ulrich, his son, his nephew, and I sitting in a circle, holding each other's hands. That's what I wish for and I have no idea how I can convince the three men to do this tomorrow.

The Final Morning

Waking up around six, I hesitate in opening my eyes. Today Ulrich will die. The hour of death, which normally is a big unknown, has been set—a matter-of-fact point in time in his, and in all of our lives. How is this even possible?

I crawl out from under my covers in an attempt to get up. My body stiffens, straining to support me in this moment of shock. A voice message from a friend who, for the past five days has supported me via phone each evening from the south of France, changes everything. She tells me she'll be sending positive energy our way. This is what I've been longing for: the support of a woman, because I have no clue what this will do to me—to all of us—today.

Feeling that I'm also in need of extra male support, I leave a voice message for a close friend of mine. In just a few minutes he replies in his warm, confident voice that he too will be there with us in spirit. Filled with humility and gratitude, I become soft, open, receptive again. Exactly what I need right now.

At nine o'clock I'm fortified by yoga and breakfast, yet I'm hesitating to go. It's still not clear whether I can—or want to—witness and accompany Ulrich's passing at ten. That is, in one hour. My free will against his!

Aimlessly I wander around my apartment, finding my way through the tyranny of dwindling minutes—until a powerful wave of clear pure *'yes'* washes me out onto the street and directly to Ulrich. Just as I lock my bike in front of his house, my cell rings. "Ulrich B." I read on the display and press the doorbell. The nephew greets me with Ulrich's phone in his hand. "Ulrich's growing agitated, he wants to know if you're coming!" he grins. I smile. Yes, this is Ulrich, this relentless impatience. Only today do I really understand it. I head straight for the living room; I can't wait to see Ulrich, to find out how he's doing.

Although I wasn't expecting anything, the scenario that presents itself floors me. Ulrich is sitting calmly at the richly laid breakfast table. Sausage, cheese, half-filled coffee cups; a few bread rolls that his son brought this morning and which are still in the basket. With strawberry jam smeared in the left corner of his mouth, Ulrich exclaims with a mixture of relief and reproach, "Ah! There you are at last!" I kiss him on the forehead, sitting down next to him on the right corner. I'm surprised and relieved to see how the three men are spending this last morning together, so in peace and in sync with each other and life. They also offer me a plate and coffee, but I don't feel like eating.

Ulrich reaches for my hand, and I take it in mine, moving a little closer to him. "How are you?" I ask cautiously. He looks uncertain. "We had a big party yesterday," the nephew answers in his place, and Ulrich agrees with a grin, "Yes, it was nice!" "So many stories and toasts! You had quite the time!" the nephew nudges Ulrich in the side, laughing. Ulrich smiles even more and my heart is warmed by how amicable the two of them are with each other.

A glance at the clock, however, makes me shiver. Quarter to ten. We only have fifteen minutes until the doctor arrives. In the midst of my sheer panic, I hear the nephew: "Listen... this might sound a little strange... but... how about we sit together in a circle and hold each other's hands in silence for a few minutes?" I'm at a loss for words. My wish! The vision I'd clearly seen in front of me last night and where I'd wondered how on earth I was going to make this happen with the three men. "Yes!" I nod, infinitely touched by the power of thought, "yes!" The son also nods and Ulrich is so moved that he can't even respond.

I move a little closer to Ulrich until I'm sitting next to him on his right side, his hand in mine; his other rests in that of his nephew's, who's leaning forward towards him. Ulrich's son closes the circle opposite him. A great, powerful silence rises around and within me. Accompanied by the sounds of breathing, the creaking of a chair, the coolness of Ulrich's slender, slightly trembling hand in mine. Every now and then I peek into the round, can't get enough of the way the three men sit hand in hand with me, eyes closed and very serious. A completely new experience for me. In these moments, a powerful trust grows in this protective, life-affirming profound strength of the masculine, and I surrender to it completely. I, a woman, hold the space with them, and they hold me. I love these men.

When it's time to loosen the bonds, we pull our hands back. No words are spoken, yet we seem to be connected in the common rhythm of letting go. Suddenly Ulrich is sitting there all alone. Is it just his insecure and seemingly lost appearance, or is it my own feelings that are calling me to move a little closer to him until I feel his body at the side of mine, my hand reassuringly placed on his. He relaxes.

"Well," Ulrich says, looking at the clock, "we don't know what it's like. Whether there's something after death. Or not. Or what comes next. We just don't know." "Yes..." the nephew responds, "but YOU, you will know soon! And it'll remain your secret." Ulrich laughs. There's so much I want to say right now, but what's happening here isn't about me. It's one minute to ten.

At ten on the dot the doorbell rings. Fear shoots through my heart. The son opens the door. I hear voices in the hallway. Then a tanned man with a friendly face stands in the entrance to the living room. His whole figure radiates warmth. Is this what a doctor looks like who helps a person to die? He shakes Ulrich's hand, holds it a moment longer and looks him straight in the eye. "Good morning, Mr. B.! How are you? How are you feeling today? We can also postpone it," he invites Ulrich with a warm smile. Another chance to diverge from his self-chosen path— and again Ulrich chooses to move on straight ahead.

The doctor, who is already retired, introduces himself to me by name. And then: "I used to be a pediatrician." I'm stunned. In my imagination over the last few days I'd envisioned a rough, brutal executioner. Instead, here I see a man exuding love and saying the word 'pediatrician' with such warmth that it brings tears to my eyes. I can't help but trust him and I'm incredibly relieved. I even wonder if he's married, notice his wedding ring, and am amused by myself. In any case, if he has a heart for children, then I sincerely hope he'll be able to take good care of the other end of life as well.

Behind the doctor, another person suddenly appears, coming to stand next to him. A woman. Completely unknown to me. A whirl of anger bubbles up inside me. Horrified, I yell at her loudly, "Who are YOU now?" and I can only just restrain myself from jumping up and throwing her out. What's she doing here? I perceive this unannounced person as an invader of our privacy, of this space of love and community that seems sacred to me and that we've just created with our hands in the circle, the four of us.

Ulrich looks at the woman in surprise. "Mr. B.!" she calls out, "do you recognize me?" His expression relaxes into a smile. Who is this woman who squeezes his hand so warmly, almost lovingly? What does she want here? Turning to me, she extends her hand with a warm smile: "I'm the lawyer!" THE lawyer? So a lawyer has to be here too? Why didn't anyone tell me this? For a moment, I fear other people will also pop up that I don't know anything about.

Her warm hand, the powerful and somehow compassionate handshake, work wonders and I relax. Tears come to my eyes as I try to apologize for my behavior. "It's all good!" she says with the tone of someone who means it. In fact, she seems to mean everything she says. Even her comment, "The way you flared up just now really impressed me. How you were ready to stand by your father!" With a big smile I admit that I actually would've thrown her out if necessary. We both laugh, taking an instant liking to one another. For me, she's now the fourth in the group on this momentous morning headed by Ulrich, along with his son, nephew and the doctor. And she's exactly the one I'd wished for last night. That today there would also be a woman here in person. I close my eyes and send a thank you out into the world.

"How are you feeling," she asks Ulrich. "Queasy..." he mumbles," ... I feel a little queasy..." "Yes, I can understand that!" She smiles warmly at him. Nephew and son begin bombarding the doctor and lawyer with questions about assisted dying. How many times a year? And when and where? In no time at all, an animated conversation ensues between the four of them—averted from Ulrich, whose gaze I see darting confusedly back and forth between the people, and who seems to be growing smaller and smaller next to me. Even with both hearing aids properly adjusted, he'll be acoustically lost in the midst of such a babble of voices. I clear my throat. After a while, again. "Hello!" I finally call out to the group in a friendly but determined manner, "can we include Ulrich here? He's the one this is now about!" Everyone turns to him, puzzled. "Yes, of course!" and "Oh yes!"

After a few minutes of small talk, the doctor announces, "Well, I'll go and set everything up next door," and he closes the double doors to the dining room behind him. I feel sick to my stomach. It costs me an infinite amount of strength to remain seated and let him get on with it. What's happening is, and remains, Ulrich's will, I have to remind myself again and again. The lawyer sits down on the other side of Ulrich with a pile of papers. "Mr B., I still need your signature." Clearly annoyed, Ulrich reaches for a pen. "With this signature here, you release everyone present from the obligation to initiate life-saving measures." Ulrich's hand trembles; it appears difficult for him to steer the pen in the way a legible signature requires. It goes infinitely slowly.

The letters slip past his pen, tilt over, like small, angular ships in the hurricane of aging. I follow every curve in his name, which is more of a jagged edge, an outlier from the curves, even though he tries so hard to control the trembling.

"And here again, please. A copy. For you." I feel sick. At the same time, I could almost laugh. Copy? For whom? The urn? "So, and here I need your signature stating that you're the one who wants to end your life and that you will carry it out independently without outside help." Ulrich snorts and reaches for the pen again, clearly at the limits of his strength. Just as he finishes, she says, "And here again please, for your copy."

With a roar, Ulrich throws the pen across the table. "I just want to die!" he cries out, "can't I just die in peace?" "This is the last paper, Ulrich," I try to reassure him, and feel like slapping myself for interfering when I don't even know if it's true. But it is—thank God. With the last signature of his life, Ulrich has confirmed that he's choosing to die.

The double doors to the living room open. A bit like Christmas, only they reveal a steel stand with two bags full of liquid hanging from it instead of a glowing Christmas tree. One bag is large, containing a saline solution. The other is small, filled with what Ulrich has always called 'poison'. "Can't you get me some poison?" he'd asked me so many times in vain during the last six months.

"So Mr. B., everything is now prepared!" announces the doctor. It's infinitely quiet. The two men just look at each other for the longest moment.

With a jolt, Ulrich straightens up in his chair. "Well then, let's go!" he shouts, leaning on the surface of the table with both hands, pulling himself upright and storming off to the left. In a flash I'm next to him and just manage to get a hold of him before he can fall, offering him my right arm. "Easy, easy, Mr. B.!" Ulrich grins. Our old intimate game.

Silently, he places his hand on my arm. Only I hardly feel him, so upright he walks beside me. Straighter than he has for months. Swaying slightly, yet completely focused on himself, he moves with obvious purpose towards the sofa, at the head of which is the stand with the two bags. And that's actually the most incredible insight for me. Having to admit how straight, completely with himself and clear he is. He doesn't need any support. He knows exactly what he's doing.

Ulrich sits down on the sofa. I help him slide his sandals off his feet and place them carefully under the table. I'm thinking that he won't need them anymore. And how absurd this all is.

He lies down. A little slanted, his head searches for the corner, and I adjust the pillow under his head, moving it this way and that. "Is it okay?" I ask him again and again until he nods. "Do you need a blanket? Should I get you a blanket?" I offer in my fervent desire to be able to do something else for him. "No," he says, as if there's nothing easier in the world, "no, it won't take long."

Resigned, I take a few steps back and the doctor approaches Ulrich. I can't see what's happening until the doctor turns the wheel to open the big bag. "So, right now it's just saline solution running into your body," he explains. I feel infinitely helpless; I just have to wait and go along with it. In the far left of the room, the lawyer turns to Ulrich with her cell phone, filming. "Mr. B., is it your own free will to die now with euthanasia?" Then I hear the most unbelievable response in my entire life. Ulrich's "Yes." And at that moment, our earthly paths part.

The lawyer finishes the short video, which later has to be handed over to the criminal investigators as evidence. As the doctor turns a little to the side, I half see him, half Ulrich, as he places a small board on the left of Ulrich's chest. In the middle of it is a clamp, not unlike a clothes peg. The banality in the incomprehensible. "Mr. B.," the doctor explains, "this clamp here opens the tube with the drug that will send you to your death. If you want it that way, you can press on it." A clamp, of all things. Other people cling onto their lives and Ulrich can just release a clamp to die.

The doctor's last words haven't even faded away before I witness the second unbelievable thing. Ulrich presses. He presses on the damn clamp.

The doctor steps aside. In a flash I'm with Ulrich, sitting down on a chair very close to his right; the nephew is just as quickly at his feet, lying across Ulrich's legs to hold his other hand.

Somewhere directly behind us I perceive his son. I search Ulrich's gaze to see if he'll look around one more time—but it only takes a few seconds before his eyes grow heavy, the lids closing, and I just sit there with his hand in mine and watch him die. Just as he wanted. "I wish for you to be with me when I die."

There's still a part of me that's screaming "No!"; wants to remain in resistance and yet is so infinitely lonely and lost. And then the other, for which I decide, and which powerfully breathes a big, fat yes into the room with every exhalation. Yes. So it is. Thy will be done.

I notice Ulrich's chest rising and falling, and then a tiny pool of water that collects in the corner of his right eye like in a cup, without overflowing. Is it the farewell he's saying inside of himself at that very moment? His farewell to this world, to life, to us, and everything else he knew?

After a few minutes, the doctor leans over Ulrich's chest with his stethoscope. "The heart is still beating," he informs us. Endless minutes pass. Ulrich's eyelids flutter and I notice every single twitch. How the rosy color gently escapes from his face. Now he's going his way. Separating his path from mine. At least I think so.

The doctor leans over once again. "Now the heart is beating very weakly. It'll take a few more minutes," he announces. I sit there with this body in my hand and feel something slipping away. I don't know what or where. Or how. I'm wide awake, highly receptive, but I don't really notice anything. When the doctor listens to Ulrich's chest for the third time, he says with tears in his eyes, "The heart has now stopped beating. My deepest condolences." I can't, or won't, believe it.

It's so quiet. I hear sighing. Breathing. Restlessness. Everyone in the room seems to want to get up. "Please!" I call out, "please! It's happening too fast. Please let us just be here with Ulrich for another ten minutes!" I don't dare ask for an hour. Without protest, everyone stays in their places. From the side I see the nephew. He too with tears in his eyes. My tears are not alone then. We have each other.

Finally the others begin to move. The nephew stands at the foot of the sofa, watches for a while and then lovingly pats Ulrich on his feet. "You were a great guy! Take care, Uncle!" Grateful and humble, I realize what he's doing. Wonder if he intuitively knows how helpful it can be for dying people to feel an earthly connection on the soles of their feet, to have hands laid lightly upon them.

Doctor, lawyer, nephew, and son start talking to each other again. I've no idea about what, as I continue to sit in silence with Ulrich, guarding. Dying is a slow and delicate process.

At some point I feel too alone and go to the others. In the meantime, the lawyer has called the police. That's how it is with assisted dying—and I have the feeling that I'm in the middle of a bad movie. A psycho thriller. But I can't turn it off. So I open a window, wide, so wide, and light the candle on the table. Whatever I do, I always have to check with the lawyer first to make sure it's okay. Because of the evidence collection by the police later.

I take another close look at Ulrich's physical appearance here on this earth, soaking in every nuance. Every wrinkle in his face, the sparse white hair, the fine lips and the rest of his still slightly pink shimmering cheeks. A glow, a gentleness, which more often than not was masked by everyday life, has been present again and again over the last five days and is stronger than ever before. I keep looking at him, the father of my heart.

Finally I walk over, through the wide open double doors, and join the others in the dining room. Back to the breakfast table, where Ulrich's coffee cup stands, half empty. Jam traces of his lips still on the rim. Breadcrumbs on his plate. I sit back in my chair, but Ulrich is no longer on my left. His son is sitting there now. I look at him from the side. I've never been so aware of their resemblance. I can't put it all together.

Intense hunger overwhelms me. I take the last half bread roll from the basket, spread it thickly with butter and orange marmalade, and pour the rest of the now cold coffee from the pot into a clean cup. The explosion of sweet and bitter on my tongue is delicious—I savor it and suck on it. How wonderful it is to be alive!

The other four—son, nephew, doctor and lawyer—go straight back to their conversation about medically assisted suicide. Whether there are enough lawyers and doctors to take care of it and whether demand is increasing. After the last fortifying, life-giving bites and sips, I feel confused again and lost in my chair, happy for the backrest—the only thing that's keeping me upright now. I tune out the sound of the conversation.

I look at everybody around the table, then through the room. Everything hurts, every joint, my back. *Think nothing, want nothing, force nothing.* That's how Ulrich used to begin his autogenic training. I immediately relax and let my gaze wander around the room without focusing.

And then—there's 'something'. In the room, right next to the double doors. I can't see it, but I feel it. At first incredulous. My head switches on. *Now you're really going crazy.* Then I let go of that thought. *Think nothing, want nothing, force nothing.* Immediately 'it' is there again. This time a little stronger—an energy that comes together very gently and slowly, condensing. It has no frame, no clear shape; invisibly perceptible like a wafting 'something'.

I don't say a word. Our language has no words for such things. *Think nothing, want nothing, force nothing.* To my amazement, this 'something' starts moving to the left. It's infinitely slow. Around the table, past the nephew, son, doctor, and lawyer. For what feels like an eternity.

When it's halfway around the table, I suddenly think that I want 'it' to come to me, and lose it in the same moment. I don't perceive anything anymore. I still look for it every now and then.

Gone. What was that?

Think nothing, want nothing, force nothing. Immediately I feel it again. Now behind me on my left. At my shoulder. A powerful presence of something that has no name, no form, and yet is so incredibly THERE. *Think nothing, want nothing, force nothing.* My right hand moves of its own accord to my left shoulder, resting there. In that moment, I'm flooded by something boundless, powerful, and at the same time infinitely gentle—a love without ifs and buts, swept away to a place I know so well. I sink into this presence, this power that, at first in disbelief, I can't help but recognize. This is exactly how Ulrich felt to me in our most heartfelt father-daughter moments.

Something in me knows that this is 'Ulrich' and at the same time I know it's not him. Because it's so much more. It's everything that made him special, and also everything that we never or only rarely saw of him—and that perhaps even he didn't know about himself and couldn't express.

Deeply absorbed, I let this force, this love, this light, work within me. How is it possible to be so sad, so speechless, and yet so happy at the same time?

After a while, snippets of conversation from the other four at the table filter through to me and the sensation at my shoulder subsides. Now I long for contact with the living around me. In the midst of the verbal back and forth, I ask, "Did you guys notice it too?" "What?" ask nephew, son, lawyer, and doctor as one, as if fired from a gun. "Well—over there at the door!" I point.

Perplexed, a little disbelieving, but obviously curious enough, they look. Except that 'it' is no longer perceptible. All four confess that they hadn't noticed anything, absolutely nothing. Is it my imagination or do they sound a little disappointed?

I ask the lawyer if I'm allowed to cleanse Ulrich's body with sage smoke before the police arrive. Unfortunately no, because even that could confuse the evidence. I'm boiling with rage; I'm forbidden from doing what is most natural to me. In this artificial scenario, I could place myself under suspicion of a crime. But well, Ulrich wanted it that way and his life-long impatience accompanies his passing mercilessly down to the smallest detail. For not even an hour after Ulrich's last heartbeat, the police ring the doorbell.

I was expecting to see seasoned, older men. Instead, two very young officers stand in the room, express their condolences and, wearing gloves, begin to confiscate every item that could've had something to do with a potential crime. Among them are the empty bags from the drip and the needle from Ulrich's arm, which are carefully packed into plastic bags and labeled. Thank God they leave the candle standing and burning.

When they're finished with their work, I ask if I can finally open all the windows. They nod. Relieved, I tear them all open. Once again I stand at Ulrich's feet and place my hands on his soles, engrossed, losing my sense of time and space. May any remaining energy that could still be lingering in his body escape. When I feel it's enough, I also lightly tap his feet a few times and bow slightly with my palms together, full of love and gratitude. "Mr. B.!"

When I turn around, I can't believe my eyes. All six of them—the two police officers, the doctor, the lawyer, the son, and the nephew—are standing silently in a semicircle behind me, and have been doing so the whole time. They've been watching me. I smile self-consciously. "There... now it's good," I try to explain the inexplicable. One of the officers clears his throat, equally embarrassed. "Um... what did you just do?" Far from being an interrogation, his voice sounds confused, uncertain, vulnerable—and so incredibly open. "It looked so... sacrosanct. Like a sacred act!" With tears in my eyes, I nod.

I'm just amazed at how sensitive the two officers are. Even now that they've finished their work, they remain standing in the room, somehow indecisive. They don't seem to want to leave. One is pacing around. "Yes... well... we've never experienced anything like this before." "Why? What do you mean?" I ask back. "Well, we never know what to expect when we get a call. It's usually violence or something like that. But this..." he suddenly whispers, "here... there's so much love here!" His words sound like a wondrous melody to which something inside me begins to dance. I bow to him and could cry with gratitude that these two men, of all people, found their way to us.

Along with the police officers, the doctor and lawyer bid their farewells. Heartfelt. Everything flows. We've shared something unique that's touched all of our lives deeply.

Our group, now reduced to the son, the nephew, and me, reunites at the dining room table. Again we wait. This time for the coroners, who are not allowed to be sent by the funeral home, but must instead be requested by the police. Ulrich's body will also be confiscated and only released to the funeral home days later, if there's no suspicion of a crime.

It takes a full hour before two men with a stretcher ring the doorbell. They too express their condolences and get to work behind closed doors. I hear them pottering around and, finally, announcing that they're finished and will now take Ulrich's body away. I feel wretched. As they carry the stretcher covered with a white cloth into the hallway and out of the front door, my eyes fall on the wilted, dried-out red roses in the middle of the dining room table. I rip them out of the vase and run after them. Down the stairs.

At the garden gate, I call out, "Please! Wait! I want to give Ulrich these roses!" The older of the two looks puzzled. "Okay." He takes the roses from my hand and squeezes them under the shroud. "No, sorry, but they have to be placed on his heart." As if there were nothing more natural, the man opens the shroud a little higher, searches, and slides the bouquet there. It's not good enough for me though. I reach for the roses myself and press them lightly to Ulrich's chest, against his heart. "There. Now it's right."

The man looks on in amazement. "Excuse me... Can I ask you something?" "Yes?" "Was this... so... was this an assisted suicide?" "Yes!" I answer him in a clear, firm voice and am completely surprised that there's no guilt or shame in that. It simply is what it is. "There is so much love here!" he adds, tall and strong in stature, and yet so incredibly helpless. Everything in me smiles.

Before my eyes, the men push the stretcher into the hearse and drive off. Onto Branitzer Square. I wave after Ulrich on his last great journey, blowing kisses until the vehicle with him in it disappears from my field of vision and my life.

Dazed and yet happy that everything's happening so lovingly, easily and freely, I return to the apartment. I still have a strong desire to cleanse Ulrich's deathbed with sage and ask his son and nephew if that would be okay with them—even at the risk of being declared crazy by the family. "Everyone's allowed to do what's good and right for them here!" the nephew says smiling, and I'm flabbergasted. What an answer! He captures the energy of free will that I've been feeling here all along in such clear words.

The bundle of sage in my hand ignites immediately, developing a powerful smoke, which, as if magnetically attracted, moves directly at a ninety-degree angle sideways to the sofa on which Ulrich died just a few hours ago. I've never experienced anything like this in any of my many smudging ceremonies. I let the smoke find its way, follow it. At some point it rises only upwards and I know that its work is done. Finally, I cleanse myself and extinguish the sage in the water bowl that I'd prepared yesterday.

The smoke and I are finished here now. Nephew and son are clearing the dining room table. Indecisively, I watch. I want to leave now, while the two men from

Ulrich's family are still here. Cleaning up and tidying the table; family business. The nephew spontaneously hugs me and thanks me, and I thank him—deeply moved and without words. For initiating the circle where the four of us held hands, the idea of which I'd received as a vision the night before. And for his place at Ulrich's feet.

I find the son in the kitchen. Washing the dishes. "Now I'm an orphan," he says with a pained grin, foam on his hands. I look at him. Ulrich's features and this dry humor in the face of the unspeakable live on. I hug him warmly goodbye and believe that we're both so shaken by the last few hours that we can only sail on the surface for now.

Ulrich is no longer there when I leave his apartment. I don't take anything with me, not even my utensils. It can all rest. I ride my bike straight down to the lake and let the cool water cleanse me, embrace me, hold me and carry me. Lying on my back, I float along, looking up high into the sky, between the white clouds into the infinite blue.

Where might you be, dear Ulrich?

Afterwards

Thursday, July 21, 2022

*U*nlike the first two mornings after Ulrich's death, I awake today with less of an aching heart; a little less wretchedness in the pit of my stomach. Those first days when Ulrich is no more.

It's incomprehensible. And true. Despite the early morning hour, my heart immediately understands what my brain still sometimes refuses. With my hand on my chest, I confess out loud:

"Ulrich died of his own free will on Monday."

"Ulrich died of his own free will on Monday."

"Ulrich died of his own free will on Monday."

After the third time, my head also relents, and I relax, crawl under the covers, cry.

Unexpectedly relieved and calm, I go on to prepare my breakfast in the early morning sun, practice yoga, and sit in my car, undecided. Where to?

With no destination in mind, I just drive. To the corner. From there, I steer myself as if automatically to the one place that is for me the epitome of silence, purity, and peace in my neighborhood—at least during the week. Lake Sacrow, located in the middle of the forest, welcomes me in tremendous silence with an almost empty sandy beach and a clear, bright blue that reminds me of Ulrich's eyes when he bequeathed his little pocket knife to me. That was just five days ago.

I switch off my cell with the realization that Ulrich will never call again. That my phone will never ring like that again. In a tormenting mixture of fear that he might've fallen again and that I'll drop everything to help him. In annoyance of having to unwillingly hear about all the limitations aging can bring. And in love and deep connection to the father of my heart that made me rush to the phone so many times before the answering machine could beat me to it. I just don't want to hear Ulrich not calling me right now. The other people in my life can reach me later in the day.

Although I'm not a beach lover, I can't separate myself from the crystal clear water today. The little fish in it, the swan hissing as it guards the beach—all this captivates me, even if I reverently give the latter a wide berth. The change between the velvety, cool water against my skin and the warm, sun-saturated sand beneath me, sometimes on my stomach and sometimes against my back, relaxes me to the core. Like mother's milk, I soak up the powerful heat of the earth. Minute by minute and unknowingly, my inner state of being is changing from the dismay over Ulrich's death into something new, something unknown. Something leaves me, shifts in me that I can't name, but that makes me pack up and move on around midday.

With my possessions on my back, I wander through the forest, across grassy glades and along paths, losing my bearings on the way. Feeling the warm forest floor under my bare summer feet—the cones, needles, and little stones that prick me—I'm just unspeakably grateful to be alive.

Anyone looking from the outside might see a woman rambling through the forest, lonely and lost. In truth, I feel more collected than ever, becoming clearer and clearer with each step I take into somewhere—and far, so infinitely far within myself. Into this growing expanse flows an intense joy; a boundless peace and a feeling of freedom and lightness that I've never experienced before. What's happening to me here is otherworldly.

In the middle of the path I stop, soaking up the smell of the dry forest floor and aromatic conifers, and my joy grows and grows. The unexpected certainty that Ulrich has arrived seems to me as incredible as it is self-evident.

I see him clearly; how a year ago on a warm summer evening in his sailing club, while enjoying a sunset beer together—the first since the 'Corona Spring' lockdown—he raises his arms slightly in the air like wings, feather light, and shouts overjoyed into the summer evening...

"Aaaahhh... free... finally free... light... light... free... free!"

What Remains?

Mr. B.!—What remains of a life?

In the end, perhaps, it's always only what we choose for ourselves. And Ulrich? What's remained of you? For me?

Countless nautical charts tanned by rain, sun, and storm, rolled together, with sharp navigation lines and enigmatic symbols from your experienced hand. No matter how much I look and listen, all I can hear is the crackle and pop of thick paper. The constant shifting of the earth's axis is making these decades-old maps useless again, and I'm desperately looking for all the adventures, all the stories that they might tell me if you were still here.

A compass also remains. A compass from your life. North. South. East. West. And everything in between. Its magnetic needle is broken, and I spend hours repairing it so it can swing freely again on the ever-changing oceans where it once served you. As if it could give direction to your life one last time.

Well, and then there are the two sextants, carefully, almost lovingly nestled in soft cloth and shiny wooden boxes. Which of the two did you use to determine yourself and your position between the horizon and the stars in the sky?

The one sextant could help me find you in the life you would have liked to live. You wanted to be a surgeon, and your slender, delicate fingers, which I've looked upon so often, would've been your most reliable tool.

And finally, there's the other sextant. The one for the life that was possible for you in the hungry years after the war. And you did become a surgeon. A surgeon of wood. You took over and grew the family business: a funeral home including a lumber business and carpentry shop. "B. Funerals with an edge," an employee of the Ruhleben cemetery told me three years ago, impressed, and I knew only too well what he meant.

Once I asked you what you thought about your life. "It's been interesting. Not always easy. Sometimes tough. But interesting." And then there were *The best ten years of my life*, as you kept calling them. With B. And as I write this, I'm crying my eyes out. I think because you were happy.

Again and again, when I looked at you in those last days, I felt this One Thing. That it is a life truly, fully lived. YOUR lived life. And—as much as I resisted—that it was complete. Lived to the very end. On this point, the two sextants would surely agree.

And me? Where do I stand now, without you, father of my heart, by my side, seven minutes away by bike? Gently I unpack the largest, most beautiful sextant. Matte brass and very fragile. Perplexed, I sort the five pieces back and forth on the table in front of me. How do they fit together? Where's up? Where's down? Where is it I have to look through? How precisely the disjointed parts of the sextant show me my current position after your passing.

I look questioningly at the sky. *Hey! Are you there somewhere?* Your silence calls me. Echo of many spoken words. "Carola, only YOU know where you stand. Only YOU know your path. Go. Just go for it!" I have to smile. Yes, Ulrich! Yes! I'm already on my way!

It's well past midnight. I turn off the light, extinguish my candle, and search the dark starry skies for you once again through the panoramic window in front of my desk. Discover Jupiter. Then Mars. Because when we no longer know where we are, when we want to find ourselves anew, then in the end it's always the stars in the sky, the currents in the sea of life, and the supposed maps that bring us a little bit closer to the still undiscovered places of our lives.

Ultimately, however, it's just this one thing that remains for me:

How you stand in your wide-open apartment doorway when I climb the red-carpeted stairs to the second floor. How you're leaning on your cane, swaying around it like a well-traveled ship around its mast. The glow from your eyes, on your face, from every pore. Joy. Pure joy when you see me. Lighthouse of a harbor that is my father and my home. And before the harbor in my life shuts down, I resurrect you once more:

We stand facing each other, hands in front of our chests, and bow a last time.

"Mr. B.!"

"Doctor!"

What stays, what lives in me, constitutes me and works through me, is the experience of this vastness, this permeability, this power in all lightness, this light, this nameless love.

When I see chestnut trees and pigeons, and when I lay my hand on my left shoulder, I think of you. I do it often, whenever I need it.

And then...
... then you show me the way home...

Ulrich

Father of my Heart

Mr. B.

Free... finally free... light... light...free...free!

Thanks and Afterwards

If I need to thank anyone, then—above all—it's you, dear Ulrich. You became a father to me late in life, although thankfully not too late! From then on, you always had my back, helping me grow into the woman I was meant to be all along. Thank you!

In your final days and months you allowed me to get close to you, and were never afraid of my anger, my helplessness, and my tears. In this sense, we accompanied each other on a common journey, even though our individual goals—remaining in earthly life versus leaving it—were so fundamentally different. With time it became less about 'being right' and more about accepting in love and being at peace with ourselves and with each other.

Then there are four people whom I'd specifically like to thank from the bottom of my heart for supporting me in various ways throughout these five days and beyond: Christine Schulze, Zsuzsa Parrag, Alfons Köhler, and Chris Seickert. You know why!

A huge thank you also goes to the people in the writing workshop, SprachCafé Polnisch, in Berlin, led by Natalie Wasserman and Brygida Helbig. During my six-months' writing process, you were a sounding board and an oasis where I was able to try out my texts and explore their resonance in you. Thank you so much!

Extra heartfelt thanks go to my German editor, Natalie Wasserman, who, because of her great sensitivity, left the tone of my narrative intact while still providing helpful suggestions.

And then there's Sibille Roth, a close friend who's active in the worlds of theater and music. We supported each other in life and in our writing processes. We laughed and cried, acknowledged and questioned each other over a glass of wine or a curry; and thus pushed our texts forward in defiance of occasional creeping exhaustion and resignation. Thank you for that!

Finally, thank you to the thirty-two supporters who spontaneously responded to my GoFundMe appeal to pre-finance the editing and graphic design of the German version of this book. You encouraged me to keep writing even when this story began to feel banal and corny. You reminded me that what I'm telling in my book is simply what I experienced. No more and no less.

In the course of the writing process, I talked to people about dying and death almost daily. Many things were asked of me, many things were confided to me, all of which expanded and enriched my writing. It's especially important for me to emphasize that I had no idea, no plan, according to which I acted in those last five days with Ulrich. Yet it was only when I stopped fighting his long-held decision and my impending loss, and instead went into acceptance, that real contact between us became possible.

It is far from my intention to represent or judge any point of view or opinion on the topic of assisted suicide—pro versus con—with my story. What I question, however, is the way people are treated at the end of their lives in our 'civilized Western society'.

Of course, we can continue to demonize, make taboo, and stoke fear of dying and death for thousands of years to come, but I believe that by doing so we deprive ourselves of one of the most humbling and comprehensive experiences at the crossroads of human life. That of connectedness, continuity, wonder, change. And for these experiences, I'm eternally grateful!

May you rest in peace, dear Ulrich!